I0626022

Cameron & Other Great Stories

Kemi Kotun

Published by Kemi Kotun, 2025.

CAMERON & OTHER GREAT STORIES

First edition. February 25, 2025.

ISBN: 978-0957385948

Written by Kemi Kotun.

Table of Contents

Cameron & Other Short Stories is a vibrant collection of short stories featuring vivid and colourful characters from all walks of life. The stories are set across continents, from a bustling hot African market to cool northwest London.

1. CAMERON: The secrets of a dynasty are exposed.

2. THE UNLIKELY OFFENDER: A boy witnesses a crime and discovers that not everyone is who they seem.

3. THE GIRL ON THE BRIDGE: The kindness of strangers...

4. A SMALL DIVIDE: A woman falls in love but must fight her family's prejudices to enjoy lasting happiness.

5. THE LAST ONE: Three females are determined that this will be the last time.

6. FACE FACT: A woman is kidnapped, changing her life forever.

7. NO SUBSTITUTE: A woman, a man, and his son... and love.

8. ABI: This young woman is determined to protect her family from further pain.

9. TOMORROW'S BEGINNINGS: A daughter is trapped.

10. THE DRIGLAIR LEGACY: A people that could take no more

1. CAMERON

Tues 4th April, 3 pm.

'I'm surprised he made it; he was hanging on for dear life. I guess the dosage wasn't enough to kill him.'

'My guess, Dr Anson,' another person said, 'is that he was deliberately given a dose that wasn't sufficient to kill him; I wonder why. Why bother doing that?'

'Crazy things happen, that's all I can say. In my career as a doctor, I've met people I never thought existed; there are some crazy families out there, believe me; this is just one in a million.'

'Do you think he'll be charged with murder?' the other voice asked.

'The Detective superintendent said he doubts it; they have to prove that the other victim didn't commit suicide after poisoning him,' he nodded towards the bed, 'and with all their money, I'm sure they will be able to afford the best counsel.'

'I'm sure they will,' came the dry reply.

***

Tues 4th April, 6 am.

Cameron picked up the phone, 'Good Morning Grandpa.'

'How did you know it was me?'

'Who else would call me this early?' Cameron replied.

'You're an early riser, son, just like I am. I'm waiting for you.'

'Pardon?'

'I'm waiting,' he said authoritatively as if defying him to disagree.

'Grandpa, did I miss something?'

'Why do you sound frustrated? I thought you knew.'

'OK, Grandpa, I didn't know, but please oblige me... it's 6 am.'

'I'm expecting you this morning.'

'I can't come. I have important meetings to attend.'

'This morning, son...'

'OK,' Cameron sighed, 'I'm on my way, Grandpa.

***

Cameron stepped off the train at Marble Arch underground station. He was still amazed at the manic overcrowding on the platforms, especially during the morning rush hour, and at how blasé and ignorant commuters were of the perils of hundreds of tons of metal hurtling down the track towards them at hundreds of miles an hour. He knew he needed to become more adept at using the trains, having schooled abroad, first in a French boarding school and then on to Harvard University.

He crossed Oxford Street and went down Park Lane, breathing deeply, drawing the cool spring air into his lungs and savouring the freshness before the daily pollution of London's traffic diluted it. His mind turned to his work, and he shook his head at how much awaited him. He worked in Broadgate circus in London's square mile, and his typical day started before the sun rose; as he turned into Upper Grosvenor Street, he looked up at the sun as it rose over the city and sighed.

'Thank you, Norman,' he smiled briefly as his grandfather's butler let him through the double oak doors, taking his coat from him. 'It's good to see you.'

'And you as well, sir. Sir Trevor is in his office.'

The door was ajar.

'Come in,' a voice said.

Cameron pushed the door open. His grandfather was seated behind an oak desk at one end of the room. The office, cum library, was a blend of antique furniture and modern office equipment.

'Morning, son.'

Cameron was accustomed to being called son by Sir Trevor; he'd been referred to that way ever since he could remember.

'Morning, Grandpa. You look...' He paused and stared. 'Your voice sounds weak. You look like...'

'What? Spit it out,' Sir Trevor replied, coughing. 'Go on, spit it out. What do I look like?' He coughed again. 'What does a 78-year-old man look like?'

'Tired, actually; I was about to say tired,' Cameron replied.

Sir Trevor shook his head a few times. 'Sit down, son; I need to talk to you about something.'

Both sat quietly as a woman brought a silver tea and coffee set and left toast, hot croissants, butter, and strawberry jam on a silver tray.

'Thank you, Karia,' Cameron said as she exited the room.

'I haven't been well, as you can see, not that you bother to come and visit.' Sir Trevor lifted his hand in protest as Cameron was about to speak. 'No need to deny it. I know what you're going to say: that you don't want any part of this,' he waved his hand around, 'but you are in this family and this business even more than you know, and whether you like or not, there's no escaping it – this is your inheritance.'

Sir Trevor fixed his gaze on his grandson and continued.

'You're my carbon copy in every sense of the word. There's no point in shaking your head, Cameron. Your father...' he looked away, 'he looked nothing like me, not an ounce; he looked more like his mother.'

Cameron shifted in his seat. 'You're doing it again, Grandpa—staring.'

'I just can't get over how much like me you are – even your build.' He closed his eyes. 'Yes, I used to look like that once upon a time.'

'It's the rugby, Grandpa,' he said quietly.

'Yes, brings back memories,' Sir Trevor continued.

Cameron ran his fingers through his curly dark brown hair, pulling it back and exposing a broad forehead, dark brown wide-apart eyes, a nose with a high bridge, and a full lower lip.

'Why did you call for me?' Cameron picked up his coffee. 'I can still make my first meeting if I leave for my office now.'

'Someone is trying to kill me.'

Cameron sloshed his coffee. 'Ouch.' He stared at Sir Trevor, 'I don't think I heard you correctly, Grandpa. What did you say?'

'I'm the one who's supposed to be going deaf, not you,' Sir Trevor replied, his fist falling heavily on the table. 'I said someone is trying to kill me.'

Cameron sighed, shutting his eyes. He opened his eyes, looking at his grandfather. 'Are you on medication, grandpa?'

'Yes, but not the type you think,' he said, pointing at him.

4

'Who, Grandpa? Who is trying to kill you?' Cameron gesticulated as if agitated.

'If I knew, do you think I'd be sitting here talking to you? I take care of my business myself—you know that, Cameron?' Sir Trevor replied, holding a white handkerchief to his mouth.

'Look, Grandpa, why don't you tell me exactly what has been going on and for how long?' Cameron looked at his watch, 8 am. 'First meeting is out the window now anyway.'

He helped himself to the silver tray and sat back in his chair.

'Three weeks ago, I went Roe deer stalking on my friend's estate in Scotland with James and Varma.'

'Oh, when did you start doing that? Hunting, I mean.'

Sir Trevor waved the question away with his hand.

'You know both MPs?'

Cameron nodded.

'We stayed at the hunting lodge for a few days,' he continued. 'Two days into the trip, someone took a shot at me.' He stopped, 'No, don't look at me like that. Bending down to pick up my lighter saved me - otherwise.' He gestured, pulling his finger across his neck.

'We fled in different directions; the shots, however, were directed at me only – that became quite obvious. I stayed down for ten minutes and nearly gave myself a hernia until James' brother turned up; James had rung on his mobile phone. Damn useful things they can be at times,' he added, 'the mobile, I mean.'

'You said "they". How many were there?'

'I don't know, Cameron. In the onslaught of the hail of bullets, I forgot to stop to count!'

Cameron took a deep breath, 'I'm only trying to help. What happened next?'

He threw his hands up in the air. 'Nothing. The police found the tyre marks but nothing else; no leads whatsoever.'

'Second time,' Sir Trevor continued, 'Olli was driving me to have lunch at the club, and we were hit from behind, just by Victoria station. I asked Olli not to get out because I had a bad feeling that it was no ordinary accident, and I was right; they rammed into the Jaguar time and time again before Olli managed to pull away, and we lost them at the lights as we crossed Southwark bridge...just.'

'It could be Grandpa that they just wanted the car; it sounds like a carjacking to me; it's quite rampant these days,' Cameron said.

'I know you'll find reasonable explanations for each incident you don't understand.' He pushed the papers on the table away from him and placed his arms on the shiny mahogany desk. 'The third time I was out playing golf. This one's a classic,' he said, shaking his head and laughing. 'It was like a movie scene; if I hadn't experienced it first-hand, I wouldn't believe it myself.'

He looked down at his desk and then up at Cameron.

'The break on my golf cart jammed. My caddy said it was checked the day before; mine is always kept separate because it's specially made so I can stretch my legs; rheumatism has spread.' He drew deep breaths, 'I can't tell you how it felt.'

He stared at his grandson as he lowered his voice to a whisper.

'Death flashed before my eyes as we went down this slope at about forty miles an hour.' He stopped and leaned back in his chair. 'If it weren't for the quick thinking of the driver of another cart who parked in our path and then jumped out of his cart, we would be dead by now; I'd have broken my neck if my heart hadn't got me first.'

'Grandpa, this is all very distressing. Why didn't you call me when this happened?'

'I called my friends because they were nearer and knew they could get to me faster. I didn't want to bother you,' he replied.

'Bother me? Grandpa, bother me?' Cameron stood up. 'I'm so annoyed that you would choose your friends over me—'

'I wish you'd stop pacing, Cameron; your shoes are making the most awful noise against the floor,' Sir Trevor said, frowning.

'—after all, I'm the last of your living relatives.' Cameron continued as he stopped pacing. 'I know that I'm not always around, but I am reachable; you would know that if only you tried,' he had lowered his voice at this point, 'but you don't call.'

They stared at each other in silence.

'I came from a poor family; we were immigrants, son.' Sir Trevor leaned back in his chair, closing his eyes. 'I take these dark trips once in a while to remember, just to remember...'

'Grandpa, I know you've been through a lot lately, but you don't have to tell me the story again. Between you and Pops, I have heard the story a hundred times.'

Cameron started pacing again.

'Indulge me, son. I am an old man.' Sir Trevor's eyes were still closed, his thin lips curved in a wan smile. 'If I can't speak to you, who can I speak to? I will carry my story to the grave. Of what use is that to me?'

'Continue, Grandpa,' Cameron said, looking at his watch. 'Meeting two *and* three won't happen for me now anyway.'

'Sit down, Cameron. Thank you.' He drew a deep breath. 'I paid the equivalent of twelve pence for my trip; the war had just ended, and even though Britain was in as much a mess as the rest of Europe, it was far better off than Poland. Your grandma and I, bless her soul, were stuck in a small cabin with three other couples on the way here. I don't know how we managed, but when you're desperate, all you're thinking about is surviving.' He drew another deep breath. 'We got here, rented a room with another couple, and took turns sleeping on the bed.' He stopped and rubbed his hands over his face, looking far away. 'They were bad times, but those were good people. The time for good friends has gone, is long past; you don't know who's who these days, you can't trust anybody.'

'Are you thinking that one of your friends is trying to get rid of you?' Cameron asked.

He shook his head.

'Get rid of?' Sir Trevor said, 'I never even thought of it that way.'

'Well?' Cameron asked. 'You haven't answered my question.'

'No,' Sir Trevor answered and continued as if he hadn't been interrupted. 'I borrowed money and partnered with Jack Polowski, that's how I started the business—'

Cameron nodded.

'—but I had to buy him out as I doubted his ability.' He shook his frail arm from side to side. 'He didn't have the guts; I could see that earlier on. I figured that when we made it big, notice I did not say if because I knew we would make it big and that he would pull out somewhere along the way, quit, and become a liability; he was risk averse. Some people can't handle success; it's not in their DNA; it wasn't in Jack's. I wasn't going to set myself up for a fall.'

'And you saw all this in your crystal ball?' Cameron asked, 'There are times when you're like a total stranger to me.' He stared at his grandpa. 'Why make him a partner in the first place?'

'Familiarity. We'd known each other from childhood; our mothers were friends – it seemed natural to choose him,' Sir Trevor replied.

Cameron sighed.

'I conned him into selling me his share of the business,' Sir Trevor continued. 'Yes, I had to,' he paused, 'and Jack dragged my name through the mud afterwards. Everywhere. That is why, up until today, I cannot show my face in the Polish community; they despised me then and still despise me now. They treated me like a murderer and still do,' he closed his eyes, smiling. 'But I showed them. I showed them all, son. I made it alone, and I made it big. Look who has the last laugh.' He laughed aloud, holding his chest as he did so, 'Yes, I had to; I mean, the road upward wasn't easy– there were a few casualties along the way, but it had to be done; it's all part of the process; it's called success.'

'Last time I checked, it wasn't called that, Grandpa,' Cameron said wryly.

'Your father...' Sir Trevor started.

Cameron's head shot up. 'What? What about him?'

'Your father,' Sir Trevor continued, looking just above Cameron's head. 'I'd hoped he would take over the business; he was never strong enough. I could tell that from a young age. He took after the males in your grandmother's family: weaklings, the lot of them, pure gutless people.' He spat the last words out.

Cameron shifted in his chair, focusing on the picture of his grandmother and Sir Trevor above his grandpa's head.

'Do you think, Cameron, someone from my past is responsible for recent events?'

'You mean your long list of casualties?' he asked bitterly.

'Yes. Like you said earlier, do you think someone's trying to eliminate me? You're right; there's a long list; it took me over thirty years to build this brewery, and it was no easy feat.' Sir Trevor leaned forward, 'You know I've never told you the half of it; I have more enemies than...' He paused, 'I guess I've become slack over the years; money has softened me just like Joel, your father. I guess I didn't help him enough; I spoilt him and gave him everything I never had: the best schools, best cars, best of everything, but I never taught him how to fight, how to work hard, how to be a good father – all the things a man should be, all the characteristics a man should have; a strong man.'

'It's rather too late for regrets, sir,' Cameron said.

Sir Trevor was silent.

'I hate it when you call me that. Here, wipe your tears, son.' He threw him a white silk handkerchief.

'Thank you,' Cameron stood up. 'Would you like a refill?'

'Pour me some coffee.' He handed him a china coffee cup and saucer.

'I didn't know you drank coffee.' Cameron said as he took the cup from him.

'Peace is now an expensive commodity; I need to keep alert,' he replied as Cameron walked over to the silver tray, his back to his grandfather.

Sir Trevor accepted his coffee.

'Your father didn't commit suicide,' he said after Cameron sat down, his cup rattling against the saucer, 'and it was no accident either.'

He looked at Cameron, who stared back unblinking.

'He was becoming a liability; he was going to shop me to the authorities for tax evasion and other things which, in my opinion, did not matter.' He drank the coffee halfway in one gulp; his hand was still shaking. 'To have an enemy within is dangerous - my only son.' He beat his chest, 'My son.'

He laughed, smacking his fist hard on the table, 'I built this business with blood and sweat for him, for goodness' sake, for you, for generations to come.' His voice grew louder as he spoke. 'All my hard work, all the suffering for nothing. The weakling was trying to destroy me; me, his father.' He placed his right hand over his eyes.

'I know these things, Grandpa.' Cameron whispered.

Slowly, Sir Trevor removed his hand.

'It wasn't about the tax. I didn't know or understand that at the time, but I found out later that my son was bitter; I didn't take care of him as I should have and was never home. Neglect, he said, neglect.' He shook his head vigorously. 'I gave him everything I never had, the very best to rival anything his wealthy friends had, and much more, and he dared to say I neglected him.'

'Grandpa.'

Sir Trevor raised his hand.

'Everything that could have gone wrong with the business went wrong, and I discovered Joel was the culprit. He was the cause. He was pulling out the bricks one by one from within, dismantling my business.'

He looked into his grandson's eyes.

'I didn't want to believe it, Cameron. There was no other way; I couldn't stop him. If he'd succeeded, can you imagine what would have happened?' He clapped his hands. 'Finished. The end. All for nothing. I might as well have just stayed and rotted in Poland at the end of the war.' He glanced at Cameron and looked away again. 'I couldn't stand back and watch. What legacy would I have left you?'

'It's OK, Grandpa. There's no need to become distressed,' Cameron said, leaning back in his chair and sipping from his cup.

'I was baffled at the attempts on my life. Yes, a long list of people would love to see me gone. I have enjoyed life, and now that my health is failing anyway, why now?' He looked down at the contents of his coffee cup and swallowed the rest in another gulp, slowly placing it down.

Sir Trevor continued to look down into his cup as if it held the answers to his questions.

'I never told your father I loved him or told you either because I never knew what love was. You have to understand where I'm coming from. All I knew to do was provide for my family, and I excelled in that area.'

He looked Cameron straight in the eye. 'You have to forgive me, Cameron. I am the cause of all this sorrow, everything that I have ever done wrong, and there are many things...ah,' he cupped his face, 'many, many things, and they revisit me in the night-time, when it's dark when I'm alone – so vivid like it was yesterday. Families that I destroyed; everything has come back full circle to hunt me by way of my own flesh and blood. I have sowed and am reaping–there is no escape. I guess my enemies got the last laugh after all, even the dead ones.'

Sir Trevor reclined his chair, leaning back as he viewed Cameron.

'I lied about the shooters, the ones that attacked me while hunting.'

Cameron raised his eyebrows.

'Oh, they attacked me all right, but I paid someone to track them down, the same as the thugs who hit my car repeatedly; they were caught on police cameras. I used to play golf with the Police commissioner. I don't want history to repeat itself, Cameron. I am a monster, and even though we have been apart most of our lives, your father made sure of that by sending you to school abroad; it has somehow passed onto you. Blood is strong.' He whispered the last sentence, shaking his head from side to side, 'What a wonder.'

Sir Trevor began to cry, deep sobs racking his frame.

'I had such hopes for you; you're not like your father; you would have run the business without a struggle. You're a natural.' He looked at Cameron. 'This is not about money. I know you're not interested in the business. Say something, Cameron.'

'You're wrong,' Cameron said, 'it is about the money and everything else; I'm just taking care of everything in one fell swoop - less messy that way. I could have waited, but then you would have died naturally, and that, in my opinion, would have been too good a death for you, Sir, way too good.' He stood up, 'I know the money is coming to me; I have made plans: I will not be running the brewery; I stand by what I've always said, that I don't want anything to do with it; it was built on blood: other people's blood and our family blood. It would truly have been better for you if you had stayed in Poland; at least you would have lived a blameless, if poor, life; you would have had no reason to murder your own. You killed my father's spirit – you told him he was weak all his life, and he became just that.'

'I don't need you to tell me—'

'Sir—'

'Cameron, don't call me—'

'I'm talking now.' Cameron shouted, stamping his foot as he began to pace the floor. 'Things were getting out of hand, but I loved my father. I would listen in on his conversations with Mike Hefton as they planned their next move to destabilize the brewery and the other businesses – yours.' He slapped his chest, spitting out, '*My* businesses!'

Sir Trevor nodded several times, a bittersweet smile on his lips.

'Yes, blood is thick, Sir Trevor; you were right all along.' Cameron's dark rage twisted his features; his eyes blazed, his nose flared, and his mouth skewed.

'I killed him.' He stopped in front of Sir Trevor. 'I waited for you, but you were too slow. I was watching my inheritance vanish quickly, right before my eyes. The authorities were on to you, but he wasn't thinking of me. He was self-centred.'

Cameron stopped pacing. 'You know how I obsess about cars? I love the outside of a car but under the hood even more – I'm well acquainted with the mechanics. It was just a matter of... well... tweaking a few things, and you know the rest.'

He sat down with a thump, almost missing the chair. His face was in his hands, and he shook his head as if trying to clear it.

'Ohh...'

He could hear his grandpa crying softly.

'I can't let you go on; it has to finish here, Cameron; no one else bears our family name. I have left all the money and the brewery to Joanna Polowski and her two children. Jack died an alcoholic, a broken man,' he said, crying and trying to reach across the desk to him. 'I am so sorry. It finishes here; everything about us, this family, finishes here.'

'What have you done? What have you done?' Cameron's words slurred as he slumped backwards in his chair, gasping for breath.

'Oh, only the same thing *you* have done, Cameron; you came here so readily this morning to finish me off. You were expecting my call at some point - admit it. Why are you shaking your head? I was expecting you and knew what you could do; I knew you would slip something into my coffee, and I let you.

It would have been too good an opportunity to miss, especially as the feeble attempts of those incompetent, unprofessional imbeciles you hired failed three times. I drank the coffee anyway because, you know what, Cameron? I believe that *I* deserve to die.'

He sobbed louder.

'If you're not here, Cameron, I don't want to live; what would be the point? It would be sheer torture for me. You're all I have left.' His words grew fainter. 'It wasn't supposed to be like this. I was supposed to pass the business onto your father and him to you but look at us. I made a complete mess of things.' He tried to take a deep breath. 'I couldn't let you live when I discovered that you were the one trying to kill me; I just couldn't. I refused to leave my life's hard work to someone intent on murdering me; it's totally against my principles, my blood or not.'

Cameron's eyes glazed over, but he could still see and hear his grandfather; Sir Trevor's head had fallen sideways on his shiny mahogany table. '

He whispered. 'I love you, Cameron, forgive me, I'm so sorry, so...'

***

Tues 4th April, 3.10 pm

Cameron listened as Dr Anson and the other person's voices faded. He opened his eyes; he'd been conscious for some time but didn't want the doctors to know. Well, contrary to what they knew or thought they knew, the money wasn't his anymore; it now belonged to Joanna Polowski and her family. Unless...

He turned his head as the door opened.

'Hello, Norman,' he said. 'What a surprise?'

'Hello, sir. I just came by to see how you were. You sound weak. It's a shock to all the staff.' He closed the door and lingered there, looking at the handle.

'I don't think it has a lock, Norman,' Cameron volunteered. 'You look different.' He squinted at the tall, wiry figure.

'It's the uniform, sir; I had to change to casual wear because of the, erm... current events.'

He strolled towards the bed, saying nothing as he emptied green grapes into a fruit bowl on a bedside table.

'Oh, how nice of you, Norman; I don't think I'm up to eating them yet, but it's rather thoughtful of you.' Cameron smiled weakly, squinting as Norman came closer, reaching across and switching off the bedside lamp.

'How is—?'

'Enough, sir,' Norman spoke slowly. 'I'm sure you know all that has happened; after all, you planned it. Don't get me wrong now because it's not as if I liked your grandfather; he made my life a misery for twenty years,' he repeated, bending over Cameron, his face inches away.

'Look, Norman—' Cameron started, his hand feeling for the emergency button on the other side of the bed.

'Don't get me wrong again, sir; I have no complaints about my position; I chose my profession and all the crap that came along with it, but you see, I think twenty years working for your grandfather deserves something, don't you? Something special, I mean.'

'I'm sorry, Norman, I don't quite follow you.' Cameron looked into watery blue eyes, his hand moving back and forth, frantically searching for the emergency button along the side of the bed.

'Is this what you're looking for, sir?' Norman pointed to the button on the side of the bed where he stood. 'This is a matter, sir, which can be sorted out rather quickly,' he said, smiling at Cameron, who stared back at him. 'Just a small matter, sir. You see, Sir Trevor made contingency plans; he always wanted things to go his way, even after his death. I'm not happy that he's still controlling me from the grave, but for what I'm about to receive, well, I'm willing to do one last thing. Your grandfather has left me some money and other things in his will; he told me the amount, sir; it's a lot of money by my standards, but there is a catch.' He stopped and looked towards the door as the sound of footsteps hesitated a second and then went past.

Norman continued.

'The problem is that I don't get the money as long as you're alive. Do you see where I'm coming from, sir? It has nothing to do with me, just Sir Trevor's conditions. I was instructed to poison your tea, but it's obvious I didn't add enough – it was my mistake.'

'But I didn't—'

Norman lifted his hand, holding in it the plastic bag that had contained the grapes.

'I don't think you meant to kill him the first three times; the people you hired were amateurs, and he knew it, but he felt that you wouldn't miss the opportunity to poison him – that's why he let you serve coffee, that's usually Karia's job. I slipped the poison into the coffee pot; I distracted Karia when she was making it. I wanted to give you a helping hand. He thought it was you who had poisoned him. Do you know that? I was listening at the door.'

He chuckled as he moved closer.

'Sir Trevor's last words were touching: *Even though I know he poisoned me, I still love him.*'

Norman stretched the bag with both hands.

'I couldn't wait any longer for my dream house on St Croix; I wasn't sure how long he would go on living for. That's enough talk for now.'

He placed the nylon bag across Cameron's face, stretching it with his elbow, and pressed down on his chest.

Cameron struggled weakly.

The door crashed open as two doctors rushed in with a nurse. They pulled Norman off Cameron, and the nurse pulled the plastic bag off his face.

'He's okay, he's fine,' she said, breathing hard. She smoothed his hair back from his forehead. 'You're okay now; I passed by earlier and heard voices. I thought the doctors were in here, but then I headed to reception, and they were there, so we came to see who it was and heard everything he said.' She soothed him, trying to get his breathing back to normal as he held tightly onto her hand, 'Security will hold him until the police get here,' she said.

The two doctors dragged Norman, kicking and screaming, out into the hospital corridor, closing the door behind them.

'It's my inheritance, too; I have worked for it. Mine, mine,' Norman's voice faded away down the corridor.

Cameron returned the nurse's smile.

'What's that?' he asked, nodding towards the new drip she hung.

'Everything is going to be fine now,' she said without looking at him as she deftly adjusted the flow and then hooked the drip to his right arm, taping it tight. 'This should help...it's just a little something to make you *sleep* very well.'

'I don't think I need it, though,' he said, slurring his words as he tried to focus on her.

She didn't reply as she finished adjusting the drip.

'I believe we should get acquainted very quickly,' she said as she tucked his left arm tight under the sheets.

'My grandfather and yours were once very close,' she whispered near his ear. 'My name is Julia, Julia Polowski.'

The End.
  Cameron © Kemi Kotun

2. THE UNLIKELY OFFENDER

Abe held on to Dad's hand for dear life as the pressing crowds almost lifted him off his feet at the entrance to the Iddo market. The population of Iddo was double its intended capacity; buyers and traders alike jostled for space.

Iddo market, pronounced 'Eddough', was in complete contrast to our residence in Lagos suburbia, where neatly trimmed green lawns surrounded white villas, and gardens were filled with a beautiful array of colours and the scents of hibiscus, bougainvillea, and Africa never-die flowers.

It was hot, simmering, and sweaty on this particular Saturday at the Iddo market, a two-mile hub of frenzied activity.

Abe clung onto Dad's arm as he haggled with the trader, the other hand covering his nose. The air was saturated with the putrid smell of sweat and grime. The market doubled as a residence for some of the traders, and so, after market hours, the front doors closed, and the shop became home.

Dad said the shop owners' living-in factor caused the constant stench —the deep, open gutters were filled with refuse washed away only by rain – when it rained. It didn't rain much, except during the rainy season, but no one seemed to mind or care, and the buying and selling went on as usual.

All the shops were built with grey and unpainted cement blocks. They had huge double doors that opened up to the front, where buyers stood haggling with the traders.

Dad haggled...

'Don't waste my time. What is your last price?' Dad laughed again.

'Sir, this shop is my life,' the trader said, his open palms lifted. 'When I give you a price, I am serious. I want you to buy—'

'I know, but I also know how much is in my hand.' Dad lifted his palms, mimicking the trader. He turned to Abe, 'Son, don't hold on so tight,' Dad smiled, pulling out a white handkerchief and wiping Abe's face with it, 'Are you okay, Abe? I won't be long.'

Dad turned back to the trader.

'Sir,' the trader said, 'on my mother's grave, I can't sell for any less.' The trader put his fingers to his mouth and made a kissing sound, 'On my mother's grave,' he repeated.

'Your mother is not dead,' a woman behind him in the shop said without looking up from her sewing machine.

The trader hissed without turning around and continued to address Dad. He glared. 'Sir, I have other customers to attend to.'

'Where?' Dad asked, looking to his right and left.

Abe watched as Dad and the trader continued to exchange words. He turned his back on Dad; the plank across the large gutter separated him from the never-ending flow of human traffic. He used his hand to shield his eyes from the sun and watched the activity in the shops on the opposite side.

A large man picked his nose.

'Yuck.'

Abe's gaze moved to the next shop. A woman slapped a man hard in the face.

'Ouch.'

Abe quickly averted his gaze to the third shop, and something caught his eye...

A tall man, Abe couldn't tell whether the man was buying or selling; the crowds sometimes blocked off his view, but he moved forward, keeping his focus on the man.

The man slipped a wallet out of someone's pocket and into his. He moved down the row of shops, hands in his pockets as he stood still, and then moved in amongst the buyers haggling, his nimble fingers relieving people of their property, leaving the scenes of his crimes behind him with a slow, confident, steady walk.

Abe crossed the plank without looking back at Dad and followed the man.

He gulped the hot air, grimacing as he did so, sweat rolling down his face onto his neck and beneath his t-shirt. He wiped the sweat off his face with the back of his hand, keeping his eyes on the tall man's back as he almost blended in with the thick crowds. Abe stayed close.

Five minutes later, Abe stopped abruptly because the man had stopped in front of another shop selling electrical appliances.

The man said something to the trader, pulled out one of the stolen wallets and handed the trader some money. The trader turned, went in, and reappeared with a box.

Abe squinted to see the box clearly and made out a picture of a table fan.

The man took it and moved on.

This time, he didn't stop, whistling and swinging his hips as he carried the box by his side.

Abe followed him. There were fewer people now as the man walked past the last of the shops, arriving at the end of the south side of the market.

He looked up at the rusty sign that read 'MARKET EXIT' and then at the little kiosk near the exit, occupied by an elderly car park attendant. He stopped suddenly, his eyebrows rising and his jaw, dropping. His gaze followed the man as he walked towards the only other building, quickening his steps.

Each step Abe took was now slower than the last.

'I don't believe it,' he whispered.

He wiped the sweat off his forehead, and his hand shook, but he walked towards the huge double doors, which were ajar and peeped in.

"The thief" was stooped, plugging in his new purchase—the fan.

With his mouth still agape, Abe looked up at the sign across the door and back inside the building. Another man had joined "The Thief".

Both men stood before the now rotating fan, talking and smiling as they bent their faces close to it.

'There you are, son.' Dad's gleaming smile lit up his face.

Abe jumped.

'I'm really sorry. That silly trader was wasting my time. I knew you'd make your way here if you got lost,' Dad said, relieved, as he picked Abe and hugged him tight, lifting him off his feet. 'Good boy, you're a good boy, Abe.'

'Dad...'

The 'other man came to the door. He addressed Abe.

'Oh, so you were lost, young man? Very smart of you to come straight to us; that's what we're here for: to uphold the law and keep order in this market.' He looked at Dad, 'It's too rowdy, you know. We must watch out for the thieves and people who come here to take advantage of law-abiding citizens.'

Dad shook the officer's hand. 'Thank you, sir.'

'No problem,' the officer replied, 'our reputation precedes us as one of the best police stations in the district.' He tapped his round belly as he spoke.

The police officer, 'The Thief,' joined him, buttoning up his police uniform shirt.

Abe fixed his eyes on the man while Dad continued to hug him.

'Officers,' Dad said laughing, 'please excuse my son. It's unusual for him to be tongue-tied.' He asked Abe, 'What made you walk away like that anyway?'

Abe's gaze was still transfixed on the officer, 'the thief'.

'I, dad, I...'

'Never mind, son, I have found you, and that's all that matters. Phew. Imagine going home and telling your mother that I had lost you; my life wouldn't be worth living,' Dad was laughing as he put Abe down.

He turned to the officers and thanked them again.

'Come on, Abe,' Dad tugged at Abe's arm, 'come on, son.'

Getting no response, Dad lifted him again.

Abe was still looking at the officer, the thief, as Dad carried him away.

The thief was staring straight back at Abe, his eyes slits, his forehead furrowed; he tapped his forefinger to his lips slowly.

The thief leaned over and whispered into the other officer's ear - that was the last thing Abe saw before Dad carried him out of view of the officers.

***

'My little brother's a hero, and I know he was telling the truth, Dad,' I said.

'I won't even question it, Desola. He tells you, his big sister, everything. That explains why he couldn't speak,' Dad replied. 'I knew something was wrong, but I was just too overjoyed to have found him.' He rubbed his open palm over his face. 'What a brave son I have. I'll tell him when he wakes in the morning how proud I am of him, and as for those police officers, I'll report them to the High Commissioner of Police; he goes to the same sports club as my doctor.'

Dad laughed out loud, 'Those thieves won't be enjoying the cool air for much longer.'

The End.

The Unlikely Offender © Kemi Kotun

3. THE GIRL ON THE BRIDGE

Beau Richmond locked his front door. The cool crispness of the early morning air stung his cheeks, leaving a pale patch of redness. He could feel his nostrils stinging as the cold blast hit him full force when he stepped onto the path. He dreaded this short walk to work every morning of the working week in the winter months. His employers had rented and paid for this small luxurious flat so he could get to work on time; there could be no excuse for being late – no commuter delay.

Beau wrapped his thick black cashmere coat around him, put on his leather gloves, bent his head, and walked rapidly; he could find his way if blindfolded.

London Bridge loomed ahead, and he breathed in deep as he started to cross it. The wind coming off the River Thames in the morning was particularly cruel. At 5.30 am, there was very little traffic, so he walked on the road as far away as possible from the rails. He knew there was no way he could be swept in, but he just disliked looking down at the ominous waves.

Head down, he walked as fast as he could. As he got to the middle of the bridge, he stopped. Had he just seen something out of the corner of his eye? He turned around, and his heart stopped for a few seconds.

Beau ran back, climbing over the low wall onto the bridge's path. He approached a figure — a woman.

The bright bridge lights shone on her. She had one bare leg over the rail and seemed to Beau to be trying to hoist herself over.

He tried to steady his breathing.

'Hi,' he said quietly.

She continued her mission to get the other leg over, and Beau knew she hadn't heard him.

'Hi,' he said louder.

This time, she looked up, startled. Large almond-shaped eyes stared at him as if he were a mirage. Her mouth was open as if she wanted to speak, but she couldn't find her voice.

'Whatever it is, I can help you, ' he heard himself say to his surprise.

He stopped moving towards her. Where had that come from? He didn't even know what he was saying. Was he trying to stop her, or was he afraid of what could happen?

'You can't,' the woman's faint voice reached him. 'Please go your way; it's none of your business.' She turned her back to him.

Beau got closer. 'What's your name?'

'Dana,' she replied without turning.

'Mine's Beau.'

He had recovered from the shock of seeing her there by now and drew closer.

'You know Dana,' he said, 'I would really like to help. Sometimes, your troubles need to be shared with others– the right people.'

This time, she turned, looking at him silently.

Beau thought she was weighing his words, but she shook her head.

'No one can help me,' she spoke with finality.

Beau's heart fluttered. He figured she was in her thirties; she looked mixed race to him, with thick black curls down her back, thick eyebrows above dark eyes, a small nose, and full lips in a beautiful heart-shaped face, he thought, despite the threatening situation.

'Speak to me,' he spoke gently, reaching out his hand. 'I won't come near, I promise.'

He touched his phone in his pocket. How could he call emergency services without her seeing – it might just tip her over the edge. He was so thankful he hadn't stopped to finish his coffee; he might have been too late.

'Dana, at least let me be the judge of that. Please speak to me.'

''Don't call anyone,' she focused on his hand in his pocket. Her voice hardened, 'Stay where you are.'

Beau would never have believed that he could sweat on such a cold, wintry morning, but he wiped the beads off his forehead, trying to figure out what to do and say simultaneously.

To his surprise, she started speaking, her voice shaky and low so that he had to strain to hear.

'My fiancé dumped me...I found out I was illegitimate: my natural dad's not white, he's black, and my natural mum's not black, she's white—I don't know who I bloody am.' She was waving her free hand in the air, the other holding onto the rail.

Beau caught his breath.

She continued, 'I've been missing work for months – stressed out, and now I've lost my job—years of hard graft —down the drain, just like that.'

Beau made comforting sounds, deciding it was best to let her talk. At least her mind was occupied, he thought as he encouraged her to speak.

When she finished, he said softly.

'Dana, I've been through worse – my wife left me and took my son, I have to travel up to Scotland to visit him, my mother died suddenly of a short illness...but I've had to pull through day by day.' He stretched out his now numb hand. 'You must be freezing Dana in that thin dress.'

She stared at him as if seeing him for the first time. Her eyes ran over his face.

'Please,' Beau said, his hand still outstretched. 'What will it take to get you off there.'

'Why do you care?' Her stare challenged him.

Say the right thing, Beau, he spoke to himself.

'Because Dana, you're a beautiful young woman with the whole world ahead of you...I know you can get past this.'

'I...I just want to get married—I'm ashamed.'

'Why?' he asked quickly to keep the conversation going.

Dana was beginning to shake violently; he thought it was because of the strain on her arm holding the rail combined with the cold. Her thin cotton dress was no protection in these icy temperatures.

He started to take off his coat.

'It's tomorrow.'

'What is?' he said as he moved closer. 'I just want to cover you with this', he said quickly at the alarm in Dana's eyes.

She closed her eyes. 'The wedding.'

'But...'

She nodded. 'I know. I didn't tell anyone it was off. Everyone is still coming.' She began to sob. 'From all over the world.' She turned towards the water. 'Lord, Lord, I can't face it.'

Suddenly, she lifted her second leg over.

'Don't, ' Beau shouted, his body shaking uncontrollably. He looked to the left and right. 'Where is everyone?' he shrieked, feeling helpless. 'Please don't do it, Dana. Don't jump.'

She leaned forward and stepped an inch forward.

'I'll marry you.'

She hesitated before turning to look at him. 'What?'

'I'll marry you,' he repeated. 'If you want to, we'll get married as soon as we can get a marriage licence.'

'You don't have to say that. I mean, you're very kind.' Dana's face was wet; her tears mixed with the sudden heavy downpour. She looked down at the choppy waters. 'Please move on quickly.'

'I will marry you, and everything will be alright, Dana, I promise.' He could hear the desperation in his voice. If this proposal didn't work... 'These things happen – tell your friends and family and whoever that you fell out of love with—'

She shut her eyes.

'Michael.'

'Yes, Michael. And in love with me— and we're getting married.'

'But—how?' She looked down at the water. 'How?'

'No buts, Dana. We can do this.' He laughed nervously, knowing if she slipped, that was it. 'I want to get married anyway.' He looked into her eyes. 'You really are beautiful...'

'Highly strung,' she said softly, with a strained smile as she turned away.

'Not so. It's the circumstances – most people don't know what they will do until they're pushed.'

They stood there silently as a black cab pulled up. Beau looked at the car and raised his palm, asking the driver to stay still.

Dana remained silent as if contemplating the offer.

'Dana, I'm stepping towards you. Please give me your hand.'

He reached out and she placed her hand into his. He put his other hand around her and lifted her over the rail.

He looked down into her rain-soaked face.

''I promise I will do what I said.' He smiled, relieved.

The cab driver stepped out and ran towards them, picking up Beau's coat and throwing it over Dana.

She looked up into his face as if drugged and hugged him.

'Please take me to my friend's house.'

He nodded, looking at the cab driver.

'Thank you for stopping.'

The cab driver nodded.

***

Three weeks later, Beau stood dressed in a navy suit, a white shirt, a lemon-coloured tie, and a matching silk pocket handkerchief. Looking at his reflection in the mirror: short dark curly hair and dark brown eyes, he wondered what Dana's ex, Michael, looked like. Was he built like him? Athletic? Most of his weekends were spent playing for his rugby club, and the others, cycling and swimming. He wondered what she liked doing. He shook his head as if to disperse the thoughts and unease.

Beau turned around.

'Adrian, if you want to say something, just do it.'

''You're my baby brother, and you've always been crazy, but this is ridiculous. You need to get this girl—'

'Dana, please remember her name. In an hour, she'll be your sister-in-law.'

'Yes, get her help—not marry her.' He sat down on the bed, his suit identical to Beau's. 'I love you... and I'm scared, Beau. People have always taken advantage of you from a young age, and I have always been there to save you.'

'Not this time, Adrian, I just know it's the right thing to do. And by the way, she has sought help – the doctor said she overreacted to a situation because she couldn't control the outcome. Apparently, she's used to being in control, but with work and other things...she tipped over the edge; his diagnosis is that she'll make a full recovery. She's a different woman from the one I rescued on the bridge weeks ago.'

They locked eyes.

'Trust me, big bro. Please.' Beau said, pleading. He sat beside his brother. 'I know you're freaked out. Fiona called Dana's family and invitees and cancelled her wedding. We're going to the registry and the restaurant nearby.' He paused. 'I've met her parents; there's a bit of an issue at the moment because she only just discovered that she was adopted—'

'You're kidding. Do you know what you're letting yourself in for, especially after Maggie – she had emotional baggage, too? And who's Fiona?'

'Her best friend. I dropped her at Fiona's on the day... anyway, she's been invaluable.'

'And—'

'Nothing. She was very calm, sweet, and...pretty.' He coughed as if embarrassed.

'You're joking, right? You met her friend and liked her instantly.' He wagged his finger. 'How long's it been? Three weeks – that's long enough to know if you're into someone. Don't even think of lying, little brother; you had that same look for months when you met Maggie.'

'And yeah, look what happened to that.'

'It's not your fault; you're not responsible for other people's choices or mistakes.' He placed his arm around Beau's shoulders. 'That's why I'm so desperate that you don't make the same mistake. You don't have to do this—'

'Ahh, that must be Sarah at the door,' Beau said as if relieved. He knew if he listened to Adrian long enough, he'd relent, cancel, and wouldn't go through with it. He'd promised Dana, and he was going to marry her. It was a matter of life and death, and he chose life.

'I'll get it,' Adrian said, leaving the room.

He could hear his sister's voice downstairs speaking to his brother and knew what they were discussing.

Sara walked into the room.

'Well, I give up the crown for craziness in this family—I take it off my head and place it firmly on yours— you win hands down, big brother.'

They hugged.

'Don't start; I'm getting it from him, too,' he pointed to his brother, 'I can't take much more.'

'How did you get time off that crazy job so quickly anyway?' Adrian asked, trying to change the conversation.

'My boss owed me a favour. I just made Director, by the way.'

'I should think so by the hours you put in and the copious amounts of money you make for that company.'

'Thanks.'

'So...' Sarah held his shoulders. 'Speak to me.' Who's Dana? And how did you get a marriage licence so quickly?'

'It takes a month, and it's almost that, so—'

'He's in love with Fiona.' Adrian said, lacing up his shoes.

They both looked down at him.

'Huh?' Sarah blinked rapidly.

'Our brother fancies someone else, but he's a knight on his white horse with a mission – determined to rescue this maiden.'

'Nothing's changed then,' Sarah said. 'Oh, Beau, what will we do with you?'

***

Beau and Dana stood before the marriage officiant.

'Are we ready?' He asked, smiling, pushing his glasses up. He looked from one to the other.

Beau looked at Dana. Her cream-coloured dress showed off her slim, petite figure, and her curls were pulled back into a chignon.

Beau looked into her eyes as if questioning her. He had taken Fiona aside when he arrived with his siblings.

'Has anything changed?' He'd asked, admiring how her fitted light pink trouser suit showed off her curves and how her thick auburn hair fell over her shoulders. He breathed in deeply as he looked into her hazel-coloured eyes.

She looked down at her hands, shaking her head slightly.

He persisted, 'No hesitance?'

'She's still hurt, but she thinks this will fix it – I know my friend, and she's fragile right now.'

They stood silent.

'I'm sorry,' Beau said.

Her head shot up

Her eyes searched his face. 'Why?'

He shook his head and walked towards Dana, her parents, and his siblings.

***

Now Beau looked at Dana, who was concentrating on her pale pink chiffon rose bouquet, her expression unreadable.

'Please proceed,' Beau said.

The Officiant smiled warmly.

'Let us begin. We are here today to witness the joining in the marriage of Dana June Holloway and Beau Adam Kulner. If any person present knows of any lawful impediment to why these two people may not be joined in marriage, they should declare it now."

The door crashed open, and two men, one in casual wear and the shorter one in a suit stood there breathing hard. They bent over, holding their knees, as one tried to speak, pointing to the man in the suit.

'He does,' he said, his breathing ragged.

'Michael,' Dana ran towards one of the men.

He lifted her off her feet, hugging her tightly with his eyes closed.

'I'm a fool, Dana, of the worst kind. I'm in love with no one but you; it took this to show me. I'm a fool.'

'Oh Michael, I've missed you.'

He kissed her and placed her down on her feet.

Michael looked at Beau across the room; they stared at each other until Beau's face broke into a supportive smile, conveying his understanding. Michael nodded.

'Phew,' Adrian said, standing up. 'I need a drink.'

'I'll join you,' Sarah said, smiling as she hugged Beau.

'Well, I suppose that's a wrap then,' the officiant said with resignation.

''Yes, I'm sorry about this; can I compensate you for your time?' Beau proffered his hand.

'No, don't be sorry,' He accepted the handshake. 'I've seen a lot in my time, and it's better this way – trust me.'

Beau nodded. His eyes sought out Fiona. She was standing in the corner looking at him. They locked eyes for a moment, and then both smiled.

The End.

The Girl On The Bridge © Kemi Kotun.

4. A SMALL DIVIDE

Tabby eyed the papers and files strewn across her desk and sighed.

She made a feeble attempt to pick up some papers.

'Jen,' she spoke into her intercom, 'you don't happen to know where the Williams file is, do you?'

'It's with me,' Jen replied.

'I told you not to take files without telling me, Jen,' Tabby shouted. 'I thought I was beginning to—'

'You don't need the intercom, do you?' Jen asked, walking into the office. Everything's in order for the meeting, so you don't have to worry. Why don't you call Nicola and go for lunch in the park? The meeting isn't until 4 p.m.

'Thanks, Jen,' Tabby said, 'I don't know what I would do without you.'

Jen's reply was to laugh as she walked away.

***

'Are you sure you've had enough?'

Tabby looked up as Nicola spoke, 'Why?'

'I've been watching you eat. You're not exactly scoffing the food down.' She paused for a while, 'You are OK, aren't you, Tab?'

Tabby put her hand up, 'Nicky, don't go there. I've been eating well, and I get enough of the "you're too skinny" from my family. You should know that.'

'How long have we known each other, Tab?'

'Five years or thereabouts.'

'That's right- you should know me by now. I'm only thinking of you. Don't go all funny on me,' Nicola replied. 'Do you want to go out tonight?'

'Not if you're going to try to fix me up again with one of your crazy workmates,' Tabby replied, biting into her ham and cucumber sandwich.

'Tch, Tch! What's with you today anyway?' She put away the remains of her sandwich and looked down at the pigeon by her foot. It stood on one leg and looked up at her. She pointed at it. 'You need to go on a diet; you aren't half overweight.'

They both laughed.

Tabby often pondered how different they were. They came from opposite backgrounds, but that had never stopped their friendship. She was tall, slim, and dark, while Nicky was petite and plump, with wide cheekbones, sparkling green eyes, and a short blond crop.

'And for your information, it's my coz's party. You know, the one with the large...' 'Nicola opened her hands wide, smiling, 'courier company.'

They both laughed.

'I don't know, Nicky,' Tabby said, dabbing her mouth with a paper napkin. 'I've got this important meeting at four, and I know it will drag. I'll be tired afterwards. Essex isn't next door.'

Nicky raised her eyebrows.

'You might raise those fine brows, lady, but I've been trying to get you to move to London for so long—'

'And leave my mum, dad, grandparents—'

'And don't forget all your cousins.'

'Yes,' Nicky continued as if she hadn't been interrupted. 'I've been commuting since I was seventeen; you know how much I'd like to, but I can't be away from my family; we do everything together.'

'I know, I know.' Tabby waved her hand, laughing.

'No excuses about tonight, Tabs.' Nicky waved her hand, causing the now two pigeons to scuttle away; they came back. 'Come out and meet people—'

'You mean men, don't you, Nicky? Why don't you say it? Men, not people,' Tabby packed up the remainder of her lunch, finally rewarding the patient pigeons.

'It's been a year since your last date—' Nicky started.

'I'm okay, Nicky, you worry too much. I'm just working hard and getting on with my life.'

'Working too hard and all hours to be lonely, I guess—' Nicky cut in.

'I'm not incomplete because I don't have a man in my life,' Tabby replied. 'Some women are, but not me.' She stood up, brushing the seat of her trousers with her hand. 'When my husband shows up, well...until then, I'm fine, Nicky.'

'Tut, Tut!' Nicky said as she got up. The pigeons were too engrossed in their food to move out of the way. 'All this poetry and all I did was invite you to a house party, not to meet the Queen.' She brushed her skirt down. 'It won't hurt you to come out and have some fun,' she continued, 'I'll pick you up at eight o'clock sharp.' She reached up and pecked Tabby on the cheek, 'See you later, my friend.'

***

Tabby stood talking to Aunty Ellie, one of Nicky's relatives. She was familiar with most of Nicky's family, having met them at many family functions. Their warmth had always drawn her in.

Tabby looked up from listening to Aunty Ellie talk about her third husband and looked straight into the face of a man on the other side of the room. She was unsure whether he was looking at her, as she was short-sighted and didn't have her contacts in—his face was slightly blurred, but she thought she detected a smile and looked away, just in case he thought she was staring.

Nicky had stepped up beside her. 'Would you rather be in bed, curled up with that, that atrocious sleepy-eyed teddy bear?'

'"Gozo", to you please Nicky, and I use him as a pillow actually, if you really must know,' Tabby replied. 'Who's that?'

'Who?' Nicky asked.

Tabby nodded in the direction of the man.

'Oh,' she said, 'Oh,' she repeated. 'Do you want to meet him?' She fluttered her lashes playfully. 'That's one of our quieter cousins. He never seems to be able to make it to any family gathering, but he's here now, and that's all that matters...'

Nicky took Tabby's hand without waiting for a reply, crossing the room swiftly; Tabby righted herself as she almost tripped, trying to keep step with her.

'Drake, this is my best friend Tabby,' Nicky said, thrusting Tabby's hand towards him. 'Tabby, this is Drake, my cousin.'

Nicky looked from one to the other, and Tabby knew only too well that she was trying to gauge their reactions to each other.

Drake shook Tabby's hand. She opened her mouth to say something, but Nicky walked off.

They stood opposite each other without talking for a few seconds.

'I'm sorry. I'm not used to family parties,' Drake began in a deep but quiet voice, 'I always want to be somewhere else once I get to one.'

'Why?' Tabby asked. She liked the sound of his voice.

'Don't know, really.' He shrugged, his hand tugging on the top button of his light pink shirt. 'This is a bit different because it's my mother's family.' He smiled warmly, looking around the room.

Tabby took the time to study his profile. He had strong cheekbones and a prominent nose. His eyes were deep-set and dark brown, with thick arched eyebrows and curly lashes. His hair was dark brown and wavy. A stray curl fell across his forehead; she felt like brushing it aside...

He turned to look at her; his lips curved into a smile. Tabby looked away quickly and back again.

'So how long have you known our Nicky?' he asked.

'Oh, five years and some. We met on the London Underground during a particularly long delay and ended up talking. Our friendship blossomed from there.'

'That's a long time for Nicky,' he laughed.

'We hit it off straight away; she's a kind, though interfering soul,' she replied.

'Oh, that she is,' he replied.

As if on cue, Nicky walked over to them, smiling.

'Are you two getting—?'

'I've got to be off now, Nicky. I have another early meeting tomorrow,' Tabby said.

'Couldn't you wait a little bit longer?' Nicky asked, smiling at her and winking so only Tabby could see her.

'No,' she turned away from Nicky. 'Goodnight, Drake; it was nice meeting you.'

He proffered his hand, smiling, 'A pleasure too.'

***

At 4 pm, Jen walked into Tabby's office the next day. 'Tabby, please take her call. Twice an hour, every hour is driving me up the wall.'

'Put her through Jen,' she picked up the phone, 'Nicky?'

'You horrible, horrible—'

'Now, now, lady, you just want to be nosy, and I will not oblige you,' Tabby said.

'Has Drake called?' Nicky asked, speaking fast.

'No, but do I need to ask whether you gave him my number?'

'I'm insulted that you should even ask. Of course I have,' Nicky giggled.

'Nicola Hopkins, did you let him ask for it first?' Tabby asked in a voice usually reserved for the courtroom whenever her corporate finance cases couldn't be resolved amicably.

Nicky didn't answer at first.

'All I can say,' Nicky giggled, 'is welcome to the family.' She burst out laughing.

'You horrible—' Tabby started.

'My turn to go now. See ya later.

***

The office phone rang at 5 pm. Jen had left for the day, so Tabby picked up the receiver.

'Nicky, no more calls, or I'll whip your—'

'Tabby? Drake. We met yesterday.'

'Oh,' she hesitated, unsure what to say, 'Hello.'

'Hello,' he replied, 'has Nicky done something wrong?' He laughed.

'Nothing unusual; I'm too used to her to let her bother me. I can handle her,' she finished.

'Yes, yes,' he said, remaining quiet for a few seconds. 'I err, I was wondering whether you'd like to go out; I'd like to take you out, maybe on Saturday, if you're free.'

She placed her hand on her stomach, rubbing it gently, trying to quell the strange bubbly feeling.

'Could you give me a number so I can call you back tomorrow? I might have to sort out a few things, like babysitting for my sister,' Tabby replied.

He gave her a number, made small talk, and said goodbye.

Tabby put the phone down and put her face in her hands, 'Babysitting indeed.'

***

On their first date, they talked about everything; Tabby listened as Drake told her about his parents, business, and love for the Arsenal football club.

'You're not as quiet as I first thought,' she said, walking beside him as they strolled along the Festival pier.

'Is that a compliment or not? I can't tell,' he asked, turning to her, smiling.

Tabby just smiled in return, saying nothing.

He bought her ice cream and a few snacks, and they sat on a bench, people-watching and talking the afternoon away.

He owned a construction company, he informed her.

'I love my work,' he said, laughing when she told him she thought so because he had a twinkle in his eye when he talked about it.

'That's where we're going,' he pointed to a restaurant on the other side. We're crossing the pier.'

'You mean there's more,' she laughed.

'You didn't think I brought you out just for a walk along the Thames and a few snacks, did you?' he asked, looking into her eyes.

She looked back, shaking her head. That strange, bubbly feeling started up again in the pit of her stomach; she placed her hand on it, rubbing it gently.

***

'I feel like a school girl,' she said, confiding in her sister later over the phone, 'I'm supposed to be a hard-nosed corporate lawyer and all, but I feel like a teenager. I can't tell Nicky this because she'd only start making wedding plans.'

'So tell me,' Ava said, 'what does he do for a living?'

Tabby had always thought her sister, Ava-Maria, had got the better of the family names,

'He's a builder,' she replied, 'Hello, are you still there? Ava?'

'Yes, yes I am,' Ava replied, 'I err, I thought you were going to say that he would be err...'

'Lawyer, Doctor. I know what's expected of me, Ava, but I don't care. We like each other, and that's all that matters.'

'I'm sorry, I didn't mean to sound that way, sis. I should know better,' Ava paused for a while, 'I mean, look at me, Tabby. I craved this fast-paced life of ferocious high-societal activity and appearing in the right places with the right people, and since Adrian is well-connected - it has never been too hard. We've been to all the usual rounds of summer parties to be seen at, the appropriate winter getaway, the countryside weekends; you name it. Do you know that at one point, my sole aim was to ensure I was snapped to appear in all the right magazines? Snapped with all the right people, but am I happy? Are Adrian and I happy?' She answered her questions, 'No.'

'I'm sorry, Ava, I always thought that was what you wanted and that you were happy; I didn't know...' Tabby said.

'When all the parties and functions end, and the lights dim,' Ava took a deep breath, 'it's just Adrian and me, and there's not much else,' she paused, 'well...we have two beautiful children, and I want them to grow up happy, well -rounded – unlike you and I Tabby.' Ava sighed, 'Adrian and I are cutting out this crazy lifestyle, ridding ourselves of the so-called friends we surround ourselves with, and getting to know each other better. I don't know who my friends are anyway,' she sighed. 'At least you have Nicky.'

'Are you there, Ava?' Tabby asked after a short silence.

'Yes. Tabby, have you... have you told Mother yet?' she asked, her voice trembling.

'Not yet', she replied quietly, 'I would rather leave that for now.'

***

Six Months Later.

'You can't be serious, Tabitha. What are you trying to do to this family?'

'What do you mean this family? Mother, you either accept him or you don't; I have lived all my life...according to your rules, exactly how you wanted, Mother. We both have.' She almost spat out, pointing to Ava, who she had brought for moral support, 'It's time you left us alone to live our own lives.'

'Stop shouting like a, like a market woman. I didn't bring you up that way. Your own life indeed; this is what you call living your own life? You're making a huge mistake. I told you years ago that your association with that Nicky girl would bring you nothing but—'

'Now, now, my dear,' Tabby's father interrupted, 'there's no need to go that far.' John Leighton stood up, a tall, silver-haired man.

'Sit down, John!' Lora, his wife, said to him.

'That's right, Mother, tell Dad what to do, like you do everybody else. You're not happy unless you're controlling people,' Tabby shouted. 'Well, the buck stops here. If Drake asks me to marry him, I'll do so with or without your blessing.'

'It's alright, Tabby.' Ava put her arm around her shoulders. 'There's no need to get so worked up.'

'No need, did you say no need, Ava?' Their mother asked. Her usual cream complexion was now a beetroot-red, her nose flared, and she waved her slender arms. 'There is a need; we are a titled family.' She turned to Tabby, 'Tabitha—'

'Why don't you ever address me as Tabby, mother?' she asked.

'—if your father will stand and watch you break with the tradition of this family,' her mother continued, ignoring the question, 'I will not. My mother did not. My grandmother before her did not. You will break off this relationship with this...' she shook her head from side to side, 'with this—'

'Builder,' Tabby finished for her.

Her mother sat beside her husband on the sofa, eyes closed, hands on either side of her face.

'Ava, I won't let your sister disgrace this family. It's bad enough her having friends from that,' she hesitated momentarily, 'part, and bringing that girl to every social and family event, but to marry into them - I won't allow it. I won't.' She stood up suddenly again.

John pulled his wife down gently. She patted stray hairs into her neat chignon and smoothed down her silk wool skirt.

'You really should calm down,' John said quietly. 'She didn't say she was getting married to him.'

'John, I just... I just have this ill feeling,' she placed her hand flat on her chest. 'I can't help it.' She looked up at Tabby, 'You had the best education, the best schools, boarding schools; we threw money at your education, much more than we did at Ava, and you want to throw that all away. Look at your sister; she married well into a titled family and is happy. Why can't you be like that?' She paused, 'I'm not ashamed to say that we expect more of you.' She put her hand on her forehead, 'My goodness, what will our friends say?'

'Mother,' Ava left Tabby's side and knelt beside her. She had the same cream complexion and the same but younger features as her mother, 'I want at least one person in this family to be happy; I mean, really happy, and you may be surprised to hear this, but it isn't me.'

Silence filled the room.

'I married well as you like to put it,' Ava continued, placing her hand over her mother's, 'and as you like to show off to your friends, but I'm unhappy.' She dabbed her tears away, her voice shaking, 'I just wanted to please you and Aunt Joan; the pressure to marry well, to keep up the family tradition, as you put it, was...' she looked down at the patterned carpet, 'was too much, it was overwhelming. You are so obsessed with your societal position that you're blind to the real thing - love, true love.'

'But your father and I have a happy marriage,' her mother said. She looked at Ava, Tabby, and then John. 'Don't we have John? A happy marriage?' she asked.

He stared down at his hands in his lap, silent.

'John?' She began to cry.

***

Tabby laughed as she watched her family help open her wedding presents. In the last six months, her family had experienced a rollercoaster of emotions; rejection, anger, sadness, and relief. The confrontation that day in her mother's living room had changed everything. It had taken time, but gradually, views and feelings began to change, and acceptance began to seep in, the acceptance of Drake and his family.

She looked at her husband across the room as he spoke to her father and uncle. He ran his fingers through his dark, wavy hair, a habit of his she had come to love. Even though he was speaking to them, he was looking at her; she winked at him, and he winked back.

Nicky nudged her, 'None of that now; both of you.'

Tabby giggled. Her mother, aunt, and sister shrieked as they opened another wedding present.

Nicky grabbed Tabby's arm. 'This must be from Aunt Ellie, bless her.'

Tabby looked at the black and white photograph of an elegant house covered in creeping ivy; the architecture, Tabby guessed, was around the mid-1800s. She took the framed photograph from Nicky. The house they were in now was almost a replica of the one in the picture.

'Hmm, does this look familiar?' Tabby asked.

They both looked over to Drake, who looked back at them, eyebrows raised.

'You know Nicky, I didn't know all those months ago that Drake had been building this dream home for me.'

Nicky nodded. ' I wish someone would present the keys to a beautiful house to me – a surprise on the eve of my wedding.'

Tabby laughed, 'I know, I'm spoiled.' She looked across at her mother, 'Much to mother's distress, we had to break with tradition on the eve of the wedding to come and see it; she almost had a breakdown.'

'It a huge triumph, Tabs, that she even came with your family. I think the size of the house, sitting in twelve acres of beautiful landscape and wilderness, helped.'

They laughed, still staring at the photograph.

'You couldn't stop crying, could you?' Nicky asked, 'You know, on your wedding eve?'

Tabby looked at her, 'Could you?'

'Frankly speaking, no one could.'

'I've never been more overwhelmed in my life, what with the wedding the next day, the anticipation of the honeymoon, and everything else.' She paused, lifting the photograph, 'Is this where Aunty Ellie was raised?'

They sat on soft, large bean bags upstairs in one of the two spacious living rooms. The front wall was entirely made of glass, and the deep amber glow of the setting sun poured into the room, bouncing off the desert-sand-coloured walls.

'Yes,' Nicky replied. 'Pretty, isn't it? Aunty Ellie is Mum's aunt by marriage, her first marriage. 'This house,' she pointed to the photograph, 'was a gift from her father. They were a wealthy family, but that's all she got; her mother never spoke to her again after she married Uncle George. Her mother said Uncle George was from the wrong end of town, whatever that meant, but good old Aunty Ellie wouldn't budge.'

'She must have given Drake the photo when he proposed to me – the house's structure is quite similar to ours. Where is it? Does she still own it?' Tabby asked.

'In Staffordshire, and she has given it to a charity for use as an orphanage,' Nicky replied.

'I guess with our situation, it was déjà vu for her - the same position she was in all those years ago. She wanted us to live here,' she tapped the photo with her finger, 'how very sweet.'

Tabby looked around her and took a deep breath as she blinked away tears. There were thirteen rooms in all, and all were beautifully designed with teak flooring and stunning latticed windows—a mix of the old and new. She and Drake had spent the last two Saturday mornings trawling through antique markets for ornaments to complement the decor. At the wedding reception, Drake's mother remarked that they would have to hurry up to fill the house with children as it was so large.

Once again, her eyes drifted towards her husband; their relationship had unwittingly started a healing process for the entire family and helped everyone face the truth about their relationships.

Tabby looked at her mother. She and her father now acted more affectionately towards each other, and her mother even allowed her father to peck her cheek occasionally.

Then she looked at Ava and Adrian, their heads bent down close together as they shared something private. They had been much closer to getting a divorce than Ava had admitted to, but both were now seeing a marriage counsellor.

Tabby sighed happily as she stared at her husband across the room, willing him to look her way; he did, his dark eyes meeting hers as he quietly mouthed, 'I love you.'

She mouthed back, 'Forever.'

The End.

53

5. The LAST ONE

I sat at the top of the three smooth cement steps leading up to our front door, peeling an orange with my bare fingers. The spray from the peel made me squint and made my dog, Jack, sneeze.

Jack was standing too close to me; she always did that when I came out first thing every morning as if she had missed me too much overnight.

Jack was a female with startling white, thick fur streaked with brown and black patches. Her name was Jackie, but that's a long story.

The sun was rising rapidly, as could be expected, along the West coast of Africa at 8 am. Jack, the birds, and I had the world to ourselves; the air was warm and moist, heavy with the tangy scent of my mother's lime, orange and white grapefruit trees, which mingled with the sweet smell of the overripe yellow flesh of the cashews. Just wonderful.

Our peace was broken by a loud clanging noise of something hitting metal.

'Bang, Bang!'

It sounded like something heavy hitting the small iron gate.

Jack and I looked at each other first as if in sheer disbelief at the audacity of this intrusion on our 'us' time and then simultaneously looked in the direction of the object of our annoyance.

The large gate for cars and the smaller one for pedestrians was locked.

A man stood by the smaller one. He was dressed in light blue West African male attire called Agbada, which consisted of yards of flowing material with complex embroidery down the front.

I walked to the gate.

'Morning Sir. Can I help you?' I asked, looking up at the stranger.

I noticed that he was holding a walking stick, the instrument responsible for making the clanging noise against the small gate.

He was tall. 'Is your mother in?'

'Sleeping,' I replied.

There was something about him that I didn't like, even though I didn't know him. It was his aura; I decided his aura was dented.

'Wake her for me,' he shouted.

I felt the pointed tips of my ears begin to warm up.

His voice was gruff. His face, I noticed, was leathery, as if he had been over-exposed to the merciless harsh rays of the African sun. His eyes were bloodshot too, typical, I know, of someone too fond of the potent alcoholic Palm wine brew or its heavily filtered cousin, *Ogogoro*; the locals called it No 1 – no guesses why.

'She is sleeping,' I repeated, trying desperately to hold Jack's scruff with one hand, as she was now barking quite loud while rubbing the tips of my ears with the other.

'I will wait,' the stranger said, looking me straight in the eye.

I kept rubbing my ears, desperately wanting to let go of Jack's scruff. 'For how long?' I asked.

For a while, no reply was forthcoming from the stranger.

'I will wait,' he repeated, eventually.

***

I could hear Mother talking to the stranger; the sitting room door was ajar, and as the curtain beads moved gently from side to side, I could just about make out her side view from where I stood near the kitchen door.

'Maryann, bring some breakfast for your uncle,' my mother shouted as if sensing my presence.

'Uncle? Which uncle? Uncle who?' I asked my sister as I stepped into the kitchen.

'Who is he anyway?' she asked as she dished *Papp* into a deep bowl. 'This is good quality corn porridge; he better be worth it.' She spooned some fried bean cakes onto a flat plate, 'I've never seen the man before, and suddenly, he's my uncle.'

'How'd I know? Weren't you listening to me?' I glared at her, rubbing the tips of my ears.

'That's right, rub your ears; I don't know why you're getting angry. You let him in,' she said in her usual matter-of-fact way. 'You should have come to ask first.'

She squeezed a fresh lime over the *Papp* using a little strainer to catch the pips.

She was quite adept at preparing a meal at just twelve years old. She was two years older than me, but it felt like seven sometimes; she was pretty mature. This made me angry, or, if I'm entirely honest, just plain envious.

'There,' she gave me the tray and turned me towards the door, 'come back with some gossip.'

I put the tray down in front of 'the Uncle'. He began to eat immediately, with what I thought was indecent haste.

'Thank you,' I mumbled under my breath.

'Thank you, my darling,' my mother said, smiling as she pushed me gently towards the door, 'I'll just have tea, please.'

Two hours later, he was gone.

**

The next day, the same man appeared at the same time, with the same way of announcing himself but with a different Agbada. This continued for five consecutive days.

**

Day six – 8 am

Mum had explained who he was on the second day; he was one of my mother's estranged uncles, divorced from his wife *and children*, as my mother had put it.

He was incapable of holding down a job, drank too much alcohol, and had lived a nomadic life for a few years since his divorce. He moved from one family member to another and intended to move into our spare room "until he got back on his feet".

'I'm sorry to say this, girls,' Mum said, 'but my family has some lazy men. It's a sad trait; in contrast, the women are strong and hardworking'

'We know that, mum,' my sister spoke up for both of us, 'but you never seem to say 'no' to them. There's a never-ending line of male cousins asking for help.' She plonked on the living room's brown sofa, 'I'm so fed up with cooking for him daily.'

'Mum, you're not helping him,' I was trying to sound all grown up like my sister, 'besides, his aura is dented.'

'What?' They asked, simultaneously looking at me.

I started to rub my ears.

Mum took a deep breath.

'My darlings, I'm sorry for the trouble.' She squared her shoulders and stood up to her full height of five feet one inch. 'I'm ready for him if he turns up today.'

'Oh, he'll turn up,' my sister said, nodding, 'as sure as Jack is going to dig another hole in the garden.'

I sat glaring at my sister. I wanted to speak just like her. Oh, she was so clever.

As if on cue.

"Bang, Bang!"

We heard the familiar sound of the walking stick banging against the iron gate.

'Go to your rooms. I will attend to him today,' Mum said, tightening her native *wrappa* around her waist.

***

They were in the living room, their voices growing louder.

'No more!'

That's all we could pick up at first; Mum's voice grew louder.

'You hear me? No more.' Mum's voice was growing even louder.

We moved closer and watched through the beaded curtain.

'You owe me.' "Uncle" was shouting; his voice rose to a high pitch, almost a scream. 'Would you throw your flesh and blood out onto the cruel streets? Under the harsh sun? To the mercy of the wicked?'

'What? You're a grown man. I can't feed you and my children at the same time. You're taking the food out of their mouths.'

'What?' he dragged the word out. 'It's just you, the two kids, and your husband in this big townhouse.' He paused for a while. 'Ahh, Rola, you have forgotten where you have come from.' He hissed long and hard. 'The good life has wiped out your memory.'

'You obviously don't know what I have been through—'

'What? What have you been through? Have you seen the way that we live in the village?' He gesticulated wildly. 'Four of us to a room.'

'You brought that on yourself.' Mum sounded like she had regained composure, 'I was like that once.' She paused, 'No, I haven't forgotten. I worked hard and left all that behind.'

He made long snorting noises.

'All of you town people are the same. Raja's evil wife told me to leave this morning. I am here, and I am not moving.' He stomped his foot like a child and then plonked himself on the large sofa.

They were both silent.

'Therese, Therese,' Mum called out my sister's name.

'Yes, mum.'

All pretence of being in our room was forgotten as my sister burst into the sitting room; the curtain beads swung back with the force of her entrance, hitting my nose.

'Ouch,' I shouted, rubbing my nose.

'Go and call Mr Ladra, the policeman who lives at Number 4; I saw him this morning while letting him in.' Mum pointed to "Uncle". 'Tell Mr Ladra,' my mother continued, 'to hurry; he knows that Daddy is away on business.'

'Yes, mum.' My sister said, flying past me.

I stood there looking through the curtains, afraid for my mother.

"Uncle" jumped up.

'Rola, you would call the police on me,' he shouted, his large hand beating against his embroidered chest. 'Me?' he said again, drawing the word out slowly.

I was transfixed to the spot, my eyes fixed on the tall, dark stranger my mum called uncle. The man had appeared from nowhere, and I wished he would return to nowhere wherever that was.

He bent down to pick up his walking stick and a faded holdall with strips of fabric hanging off it, a broken zip, and one handle.

As he rushed towards the door where I stood, his foot caught on the edge of the beige rug.

The holdall launched into the air towards me, barely missing my head as "Uncle" headed towards the floor, arms flailing about as he tried to break his fall.

He lay there for a few seconds panting, then got up, first onto his knees and then onto his feet, looking around for his holdall. His eyes settled on it and then on me.

I stood very still, as still as Jack when she's caught red-handed, digging holes in the garden.

Much to my relief, my mother appeared beside him. 'I will get your holdall, uncle.'

He pushed by her, walked over to where I stood and picked up the holdall.

'This is not the end, Rola.' He shouted. 'You have mistreated me. I will let the whole village know how you called the police on me.'

He turned around and ran down the steps leading outside.

We both followed him and watched as he covered the ground at an unnatural speed to the gate without using his walking stick, with Jack barking at his heels.

He stopped when he reached the small gate, waving his walking stick. 'Everyone will hear Rola, everyone. Wicked woman, you are a wicked woman.' He shouted as he spat on the ground and promptly disappeared.

My sister came out from the side of the garage.

'Phew. Breakfast minus one,' she said.

My mum laughed, putting her arms around us and pulling us close as we walked towards the steps leading to the house.

Jack was still barking at the gate.

'Have I told you both how proud I am of you? Your father walked out on us, but we're fine, and everything is going to get better from now on. You're both wonderful and brilliant girls, and I love you so much,' Mum kissed us both in turn.

'For years, I have been trying to pluck up the courage to say 'no' to the lazy men in my family, and finally, it's my two favourite people in the world who gave me the courage to do just that. From now on, I will just say no.'

'No,' my sister repeated, laughing.

'No,' I echoed her.

'By the way,' I said, addressing my sister as we walked through the door. Jack had given up barking at the gate and was now licking my hand, 'how did you know not to go and get the policeman?'

'His name is Mr Tadra, not Ladra, so I figured Mum didn't want me to get him.'

My ears tips were burning again. Oh, I was so mad!

The End.

The Last One © Kemi Kotun.

6. FACE FACT

The woman was swift, moving from customer to counter and back again. Every so often, she brushed her overgrown fringe away from her eyes as she bent down to take orders. She dropped her notepad into the pocket of her coffee-stained apron and rested her elbows on the counter.

'Phew. Rest, at last, Mike...'

'Only for a second, Cherie,' Mike replied as he looked across the cafe, 'that fella in the corner is beckoning with his eyes.'

Cherie turned to look at a man who sat with his elbows on the table, fingers intertwined, looking directly at her.

'I must have missed him,' she said, pushing herself away from the counter.

She stood in front of him, pencil poised over her notepad.

'What can I get you?'

'An espresso, please,' the man said.

'Certainly,' she said, hesitating. 'Anything else?'

He shook his head.

She hurried back to the counter.

'Has he got the bluest eyes you've ever seen or what?' A voice whispered behind her.

'Oh, Maggie. You made me jump,' Cherie said.

'Huh, huh, he's gorgeous; let me serve his order,' Maggie elbowed Cherie gently in the back.

'I didn't notice his eyes, and no, you can't. Go and serve your customers,' she replied.

'Something wrong, Cherie?' Mike asked, smiling at her.

'No, Mike, I'm fine, just a bit tired. Just pass me the order.'

***

Cherie walked up Golders Green High Street in northwest London towards the North End Road junction and stopped dead in her tracks. The man from the café leaned against the corner railing.

'Hi, my name's Richard. Call me Rich. You certainly work long hours. I've been hanging around, waiting for you to finish, and my feet are aching.'

'Why?' she asked, looking at him, her eyes narrowing.

'Why do you think? What's your name?' he asked, smiling at her as they approached the pedestrian lights. 'You know mine.'

'Why would I tell a stranger my name?' she asked, tilting her head back to look up at him.

'I could find out easily enough, but I thought I'd ask you first,' he replied, smiling.

She quickened her steps and then began a slow run.

'That's my bus,' Cherie said as she crossed the road and got on the bus without looking back.

***

Cherie opened the front door to her flat in Willesden Green and threw her handbag on the sofa, narrowly missing her cat.

'Hey, wake up sleepy, Mama's home. She laughed as her cat yawned and stretched. 'Mama's been busy working hard, Brinny. What have you been doing all day?'

She sat on the couch, stroking his head as he curled up in her lap.

'Another lonely evening on our own, huh? Just the two of us for dinner.'

She picked up the remote control, switching on the TV.

'I'll watch the news and then rustle up something to eat.'

***

The following morning, Cherie fed Brinny and made herself some scrambled eggs on toast.

She put on her brown uniform, threw on a lightweight jacket, and pulled her hair into a ponytail.

Cherie bent down and picked Brinny up.

'Please, please stop scratching the sofa, Brinny,' she said, stroking his head. 'I know it's like asking you not to purr, but Mrs Tandy, the landlady, is unhappy with us.'

The doorbell rang.

'Oh, my goodness, Brinny,' She kissed his head, 'I wonder who that could be at this time of the morning.'

Still holding Brinny, Cherie opened the front door.

'Yes?' she asked the stranger standing there.

He rushed towards her, and she instinctively dropped Brinny; his high screech penetrated her thoughts as darkness enveloped her.

***

'She's waking up; both of you clear out.'

Cherie heard a man's voice say.

The same person addressed her. 'Would you like some water, Cherie? It will help get rid of that acrid taste in your mouth.'

'Get your hands off me,' Cherie screamed.

'I'm trying to stop you from—you will fall off the couch.' He spoke roughly.

She raised her hand as if to cover her face.

'What's that?' Cherie asked. 'That sound, what is it?'

'It's a fan. Don't be afraid; open your eyes,' the man continued, his fingers gently lifting her face. 'That's much better, Cherie.' He paused, shaking his head. 'Uncanny, truly uncanny, don't you think so, Rosa?' He drew a deep breath. 'As if she were cloned.'

'Don't get too excited about the girl, Antonio, my love; you know what jealousy does to me, hmm...you know,' Rosa purred, her voice raspy.

'Calm down, my love, absolutely nothing to be jealous of; I'm excited about one thing only – the plan's back on track,' he replied, still looking over Cherie's features.

Antonio turned his wooden chair around to face Cherie and sat down, legs akimbo, arms resting on the back of the chair in front of her.

She shifted and looked away. He touched her face again, but this time she flinched.

'Oh, it's okay; we need you, and like I said, I won't hurt you. You're vital to the success of *our* plans,' he leaned back as he finished his sentence.

Cherie stared at his face, his cold smile sending shivers down her spine. She studied his features: his teeth were a brilliant white, his dark eyes almost black, as they caught the light from the single bulb above, high cheekbones, a short straight nose, and a full lower lip.

Rosa coughed twice.

Cherie turned her attention to the woman called Rosa.

Rosa stood by the only exit, arms crossed over her breasts, eyes levelled on Cherie. She wore tight white ski pants that stretched across her hips and an equally tight blouse; her long, straight blond hair flowed down her back. She was tall, almost as tall as the man called Antonio.

'Let me explain this to you as simply as possible,' Antonio said. 'You're going to make a video for us. I mean, you will be *in* a video that we will record; the only thing is, you will not be Cherie in this video. You will be this woman.'

He reached out, and the woman, Rosa, placed a 10x8-inch photograph into his hand. He lifted it before Cherie, holding it on either side with his thumb and forefinger.

Cherie stared at the photograph, her eyes widening.

'See what I mean?' Antonio said, 'I see you are surprised too.'

Cherie didn't reply.

'It's you, Cherie!' Antonio said.

She looked directly into his face.

'Well, almost...' he continued.

'She's beautiful, isn't she?' Rosa came closer and took the photograph from Antonio. 'There's very little change to be made, Antonio.' She pointed at Cherie. 'Her hair colour is almost the same; I will soften her hair, make it into ringlets, and then go quite heavy on the eye makeup.'

'Yes,' Antonio agreed. 'The black sequined dress would cling in all the right places.' He took Rosa's photograph back and looked at it. 'We might have to use something for her, err...'

Rosa laughed.

'It's okay, Antonio; it's sorted. We need all that lovely jewellery to nestle properly in her cleavage; there must be absolutely no difference.'

'You're right, my love. There must be no cause for doubt,' he agreed.

'Why?' Cherie asked, looking at Antonio. 'Why do you want me to impersonate this woman, and where is she?' When neither answered, she repeated the question, 'Where is she?'

'Stop shouting. The less you know, the better your chance of survival.' He put the photograph down. 'You'll be paid very well.' He laughed, 'Surprised? We know you need the money, Cherie. We've been watching your every move and know your business inside out.' He laughed wryly. 'Many bills will get taken care of, no?' He laughed. 'Oh yes, they will be,' he answered his own question.

Cherie gasped, sitting back on the sofa, her mouth ajar. She reached for the glass of water.

'You still haven't answered my question,' she said between sips.

There was no reply, and she looked over the rim of her glass at the small window with the iron bars across it; she could see that they were just below street level, but there were no sounds. She looked down at her watch; it was 12 noon.

'Are you listening? We have no time to waste. You have to be in on this one hundred per cent because you have to be convincing; we have to film and retake until we're satisfied,' Rosa said, sitting beside her. 'Then you will name a bank; give us a name, preferably not your real name – for your safety, we don't want you linked to this, but if you should be... well. We will open an account and pay the money. We'll create identity documents so you can withdraw it. I can assure you that it will be a lot of money for such an easy job.' She looked into Cherie's eyes. 'I need not tell you what will happen should you go to the police. We got you once...' she spread out her hands, 'need I say more?'

'What,' Cherie asked, staring her straight back in the eye, 'do you want me to do?'

***

'Just one last take,' Antonio said.

Hours later, Cherie looked around the basement, which had been transformed into a temporary film studio. There were lights, a camera, and Antonio—now a director.

'This is the final take,' Rosa addressed Cherie with her face so close that she almost touched her. 'No mistakes,' she said, eyes staring.

Cherie shifted in her seat, pulling at the black sequined dress she had changed into. She wrinkled her nose.

'Bear the odour; it's only for a while–it's just blood.' Antonio had said earlier. He had laughed at her reaction, 'And stale perfume. Ah, has my Rosa not outdone herself, though? You look bruised and battered enough to be convincing, and with the soft ringlets and the diamonds—*you are the Contessa.*'

'And action,' Rosa said for the twelfth time.

Cherie bit down on her lip and began to speak into the camera. She held up a newspaper she had been handed at the start of the recording to prove the day's date. She read from notes held up by Antonio.

"Michael, I'm alive but not so well." She shook her head slowly from side to side. "It has been 4 days." She hesitated, lowering her voice to sound weak. "Please pay the ransom for my sake. Don't get the police involved. These people are not joking, they mean business.'

She stopped, bending her head and, at the same time, using her blood-splattered hand to push away matted hair from her face. The rings on her fingers sparkled under the camera lights.

"They don't want anything from me but raw cash; as you can see, I still have all my jewellery on. Help me, Michael, please help me." Her voice began to fade away. "Please do as they say; they are running out of patience."

She started to cry quietly at first and then louder until she wailed.

'That's a wrap,' Rosa said with a flourish.

***

'I tell you, she is the one,' the detective told his boss. 'I saw her up close, and I even spoke to her; she is the *one*,' he said, banging his fist on the desk.

'All right. All right. Keep your voice down, Richard. Don't forget this is classified,' his boss said. 'I don't think we should tell *them* yet,' he pointed upwards with one finger, 'if you know what I mean, we need to be certain, and I mean dead certain. This is a matter of international importance, so we cannot afford to mess up.' He tapped his pen on his shiny mahogany desk. 'Why don't you use some more of that pretty blue-eyed boy charm on her and get closer? What is she calling herself?' He looked at him over the top of his horn-rimmed glasses.

'Cherie. She works in a café as a waitress in Golders Green,' Richard replied. 'But she didn't show up for work. I went there again this afternoon.'

'A waitress, did you say? Unbelievable.' He chuckled, 'It's either things are very hard for her, or she considers it a good cover.'

'I don't know, sir; she didn't seem suspicious of me at all.'

'And no mistakes, young man, we can't afford to make any; besides, this is a good opportunity to make a name for yourself with Interpol. You will be highly rewarded.'

***

Cherie opened her eyes, blinking for a couple of seconds and breathing in deeply. The familiar smells of her flat invaded her consciousness as her vision cleared. She looked at the luminous hands of her bedside clock: 7:15 p.m.

Brinny stood with two front paws on Cherie's chest, licking her face. She lifted her right hand and stroked his head.

'What a dream, Brinny, what an incredible dream.' She giggled as she tried to push herself onto her elbows.

'It was no dream, Cherie,' a voice said from the bottom of the bed. 'Something did happen, and I hope for your own sake that you remember what.'

Cherie shot up, losing her balance and falling off the bed.

'Who the hell are you? What do you want from me?' she shouted as she picked herself up off the floor, ignoring his outstretched hand. 'I can get up myself. What are you doing in my flat? I am sick and tired of this nonsense. Leave me alone, or I will call the police.'

'Take it easy now; you're not a hundred per cent okay yet; you're slurring your words. You were drugged.'

'What do you mean? Who cares?' She sat down on the bed with a thump, falling backwards, as Brinny started licking again.

'Should I feed your cat? I think he's hungry.'

'No,' she replied, rubbing her eyes. 'It's you. Did your friends send you to watch me? Speak.' She glared at him.

As she sat up, she looked down at her clothes. She crossed her hands over her chest, tugging down on her vest.

'I don't know where these clothes are from,' Cherie glanced around the room. 'Where is my uniform? The brown cotton dress?'

'I need to get you out of here and fast, Cherie. Please don't ask questions until we're outside,' Richard said, taking her arm.

She pulled away. 'I'm not going—'

'Please.' He looked her straight in the eye with a serious expression. 'Please,' he repeated softly, this time.

Something in his expression arrested her because she stopped resisting and let him lead her outside.

Outside in the dark, she leaned on the fence at the back of the house, taking deep gulps of the cool evening air.

He stood on tiptoe, taking out the bulb above the back porch.

'I'm here to help you,' Richard began. 'No, please hear me out. I had nothing to do with whatever happened to you today. I was waiting outside for you in my car, and I saw this black van pull up, and to my astonishment, they carried someone out. I knew it was you because you were not at work, so I came here. I thought you were dead but figured that *they* wouldn't risk bringing a body back. That would have been too stupid.'

'How do you know where I live?' She asked, looking him up and down in the faint light. 'And why should you care? No one else does,' she added under her breath.

'There's no time to answer all your questions,' he said, suddenly switching to Spanish. 'Tell me what happened today, and I mean everything.'

'You speak my language, ' she stared at him, and he nodded. Then, she began to narrate her ordeal.

When she finished, Richard spoke.

'The woman you were supposed to be impersonating was a very wealthy Italian called Contessa Marissa de Torrelli; she was staying in Britain attending the usual round of elite summer parties. The Contessa left to attend the Serpentine Gallery summer party but never arrived; both she and her hired chauffeur. She has been missing for the past four days; the kidnappers warned her husband not to contact the authorities, but his close friend, the Ambassador, has contacted Special Branch.' He shook his head, 'Please don't ask me how I know these things; I will explain later.' He took his jacket off and placed it on her shoulders.

'Thank you,' Cherie said.

Richard continued. 'Her husband, Conte Michael de Torrelli, was told by Special Branch to demand a video and not a still picture of her before paying the ransom. He told her to hold up a newspaper with today's date on it to prove she's still alive, but,' he said, looking into her eyes, 'she is obviously not.'

Cherie nodded and closed her eyes.

'By the sound of it,' Richard continued, 'they never intended to return her alive. I wonder how they found you,' he said, reverting to English.

'They must have come into the coffee shop,' Cherie replied. 'Many people pass through there. I think they've been watching me for some time; it all fits together now if you say they never intended to return her alive - I was supposed to be part of their plan all along; the man called Antonio said something like, "We are back on track now" to the woman Rosa.'

'From your description of him, he sounds like her chauffeur, and,' he said, trying hard to contain his laughter, 'and they figured you could use the money.' This time, he laughed aloud.

Cherie folded her arms, staring at him.

His laugh subsided, and he turned to look into her face.

'Which name did you give them to open the bank account with?' he asked.

'Agatha .M. Rossetti,' she said quietly.

He caught his breath.

'No jokes, please.' He rubbed his hands over his face, 'Which name did you give them?' He repeated the question quietly.

She repeated the same answer.

'Let's go back inside. You must pack your belongings very quickly, and I mean the *bare* essentials,' Rich spoke rapidly, grabbing her arm.

Cherie didn't move, 'Why is your voice so hoarse? You haven't yet told me your *real* name.'

'You know all you need to know; keep calling me Rich,' he replied.

'You mentioned Special Branch; if you work for them, I'm not going anywhere with you,' she stabbed her index finger into his shoulder, 'and if you try anything, I'll scream.'

'I do, and I don't,' he said slowly, 'but I can assure you that we're not going anywhere near Special Branch or any of the authorities. I'm definitely not going there anymore.'

He moved closer, held her arms on either side and spoke quietly in her language again, almost whispering.

'It was a race to find you first; they have been looking for you for two years. I was assigned your case a couple of months ago after waiting for it for so long.' He breathed deeply, 'Your father assigned me to look for you three years ago. My allegiance is to your father.'

'So, this kidnapping had nothing to do with you?' she asked, searching his features as if daring him to lie.

'Nothing, Agatha, can I call you that?'

She nodded, 'Why not, since you know it's my real name.'

'It was pure coincidence, but it was perfect.' He gripped her arms tighter. 'Can't you see? We can use it to our advantage.' He paused. 'Why did you give them your real name?'

'I thought they were going to kill me just like the Contessa, and I figured that if I gave them my real name, the authorities *and* my father would track them through the bank account somehow they paid the money into; I thought that at least I'd be leaving a clue. You cannot make a name like that up,' she said, 'I can assure you that they definitely did not know who I was.'

'Fine,' Richard said, 'we have to get out of here fast. Pack a small bag and destroy all your documents; I have new passports and other IDs.'

'I'm not going anywhere without Brinny,' she said, hand on her hips.

'Okay,' he said, squeezing his eyes shut and shaking his head. 'Brinny can come.'

***

'How long since Richard last checked in?' Sir Steven asked.

'Twenty-four hours, sir, and the woman, Cherie, is missing too,' Simpson replied.

'And he positively identified her as Rossetti?'

'Yes, he was sure about it and quite annoyed that I didn't believe he could find her so easily because all the others had tried unsuccessfully for almost two years.'

Sir Steven sat forward; fingers intertwined on his mahogany desk.

'There was a sighting of her brother and father in Spain three weekends ago; they are like moles, these people; our finest have lost the trail several times. They have gone underground ever since. The Rossetti "Family" have a network in every port only too willing to shelter and protect them, people in every continent that pay allegiance to the...' The head of the department let his words drift as he spoke, looking at Simpson.

'Sir, please...' Simpson's face turned red, his voice rising, 'Richard is loyal and trustworthy; I know him; he cannot be bought; he would never work for both sides no matter what.'

Sir Steven didn't have time to reply, as his secretary knocked and entered with a package. She handed it to him. He took the pair of gloves she offered, opened the package, and examined the contents before throwing it across the desk to Simpson.

'Well, it seems someone got to her before we did. A woman of the same height was found in a field outside Hertfordshire beyond recognition. They found this brown work uniform nearby; it's intact, funny enough. It fits the description of the one Rossetti wore at work.'

'The body, sir, how about DNA?' Simpson began.

'Forget it; the pathologists are scientists, not miracle workers; her teeth are also gone; removed. Well, it seems now,' Sir Steven stroked his grey moustache, 'we've lost our trump card to draw her family out into the open, and we were so close.'

'At least it shows that not everybody is in allegiance to her "Family", sir; someone out there still hates them enough to have tracked her down after all these years. They are as intent on wiping out the Rossetti's one by one, just as others are to protect them,' Simpson said.

Sir Steven nodded. 'Yes, you could be right. On a separate note, the other pressing case is the kidnap of Contessa Torrelli. We checked all new bank accounts opened today in case the kidnappers of the Contessa were stupid enough to open one; I've seen a lot of dumb criminals in my time, Simpson. Anyway, we discovered someone had opened an account this afternoon, not the Contessa's kidnappers, but an account for "Agatha Maria Rossetti", knowing she would never use her real name herself. Amazing. Do you think that the money they deposited means anything – it's quite a substantial amount, even by Rossetti standards?'

Simpson shook his head in reply. 'Nothing that I can think of, sir.'

'Probably just a slap in her father's face to antagonise him,' he continued, picking up his smoking pipe and hitting it on the desk. 'If Richard Cudlow doesn't show up, then I'm sorry...' his voice drifted. 'He would be yet another casualty in the fight against international organised crime. Next time, we'll be more cautious. These things are to be expected.' He finished on a high note.

'Yes, sir.'

'What's the latest on Contessa Torrelli?'

'The ransom has been paid against our will, sir. The videotape sent by the kidnappers has been analysed; the specialists say that she is the one in the video and that she was still alive this afternoon. We're waiting for the kidnappers to make contact.'

'Hmm. It's tricky: the kidnappers now have what they want, but if the ambassador and the Conte want it that way, keep me updated.'

'Will do, sir.'

Sir Steven put his head down into his paperwork.

Taking it as a dismissal, Simpson left.

***

Cherie sighed, wondering whether Brinny was comfortable. She was happy they were travelling together; she had no idea how that had been arranged so fast. Father again, she thought.

'Octopus tentacles,' she whispered under her breath; he could exert his power all around the globe.

She couldn't wait to be reunited with her mother, sister, brother, and even her father.

'I have forgiven my family,' she told Richard as they waited for their flight to Puerto Rico, both wearing disguises. 'Three years on my own is a very long time, and very lonely too; I couldn't make friends or trust anyone. I guess Interpol were waiting for me to flush my family out into the open.'

'Your family has been on the move, Agatha, fleeing the other *family*. The authorities are only interested in your father because they want to use him to flush out his enemies, but he won't cooperate with them. The disagreement between them has somewhat tempered over the last year, but it's still not completely safe,' Richard had replied. 'Time will tell how this is settled.'

Now, she sighed as she pushed further down into her seat, looking away from the window to the person sitting two seats away from her in the centre aisle. She winked, and the man returned a blank stare.

Christian was his name, not Richard. He was dark-haired and brown-eyed, and the stunning blue eye contact lenses and blond hair were gone.

Agatha continued to gaze at him, and he looked away, smiling as he did so.

'Your father would disapprove,' he had said earlier, as if embarrassed by her attention.

'What Papa thinks doesn't matter; he caused our family a lot of pain. We're all scattered abroad because of one greedy deal going sour,' she had replied.

She thought as she settled back into her seat, closing her eyes, how strange it had worked out with the kidnappers and the Contessa.

Suddenly, she opened her eyes, 'Or had it?'

The End.

Face Fact. © Kemi Kotun

.

7. NO SUBSTITUTE

Geraldine packed up for the day after her pupils had left, amazed at how much she thoroughly enjoyed teaching the Year One class.

A year ago, she had decided to ditch supply teaching and seek a permanent role; she wanted to purchase a home and "show some semblance of settling down", as her mother had politely put it.

Her love for travel had always been a factor in her employment - the ability to pack a bag at a moment's notice and head off to near and far destinations. She was the envy of her friends who worked in the City of London, with their high-paying jobs, benefits and bonuses, but they were always accompanied by their mobile phones and laptops when they managed to get away. That was Geraldine's worst fear, but... she needed a nest, and to be honest, travelling wasn't cheap, even though she had made a good amount of money from her travel blog to fund it.

She looked around the classroom to ensure everything was in place and switched off the lights.

***

Geraldine stopped at the Supermarket on her way home, driving her black Audi A3 into the parking lot. She had scrimped and saved for it and was proud of her shiny car.

Tonight, she was going to cook herself a lovely meal – she fancied a Lasagne.

'Yum,' she said as she picked up the needed ingredients through the aisles.

'Hello, Miss Bray,' a voice chirped.

Geraldine looked down.

'Toby,' she said, bending down and ruffling the boy's hair. 'What a surprise,' she added, laughing as he grinned at her, a tooth missing from the top row.

'That's my dad, Miss,' he said, pointing to a man who had his back to them; he was staring intently at the variety of bottled Bolognese sauces.

'It can all be a bit daunting,' she said as she moved to his side, holding her basket and Toby with the other hand.

'Hmm,' he said, turning towards her and staring at her for a few seconds before looking down at his son, who was holding her hand.

'The sauces,' she replied. 'Personally, I like that brand, the one with the green packaging.'

'Dad,' Toby said, looking up at his father, 'this is my new teacher. I told you about Miss Bray.'

'Oh, my apologies. I was wondering why my son's holding on to a stranger,' he said, sticking out his hand, but both her hands were full, and Toby wouldn't let go.

'Toby, let go of Miss... sorry,' he laughed.

'Bray.' Both Toby and Geraldine said simultaneously. 'But please call me Gerry. My name is Geraldine.' She continued.

'Okay,' he said, shaking her hand as Toby finally let go. 'My name is Joel, Joel Anson.'

'I've been teaching Toby for a few weeks now, so we're getting to know each other, aren't we, Toby?' she asked, looking at him and smiling.

He grinned, and her heart melted; it happened every time she looked at one of her little pupils; she loved every child she taught without exception.

'Yes, we have Gerall...' He screwed up his freckled face as if in deep concentration, a thick lock of brown hair falling forward onto his temple.

Gerry thought he needed a well overdue haircut; she remembered how, in the classroom, he was constantly pushing the lock out of his eyes.

'Don't be cheeky now, Toby,' his dad said. 'Miss Bray to you.'

Gerry laughed.

'Let me not delay you any longer.' She saw that he was about to protest. 'No, it's alright; I must finish shopping anyway.'

She bent down. 'Bye, Toby. Be a good boy, and I'll see you tomorrow.'

Joel Anson and his son said something and waved goodbye.

***

One Month Later

'Okay, kids, hand in your exercise books.'

Geraldine smiled at each of them as they passed their little exercise books to her. She spent the last fifteen minutes of the end of the school day discussing what they would be doing over the weekend.

The school bell rang, and there was a rush for the door with an echo of "Bye Miss" from some, as others completely forgot to say goodbye in their excitement to leave.

***

That evening, she pushed open her front door, keys in her mouth, hands full with her handbag and the school work she had brought home.

She kicked off her shoes, switched on the TV, and rustled up a quick pasta and salmon dish. She settled on the soft rug with her back against the sofa.

She reviewed her pupils' work, awarded marks, and then came to Toby Anson's.

Gerry read and re-read his work, and that nagging feeling returned; she had experienced this same feeling with another pupil in another school and realised it was a mistake to ignore.

She put Toby's book down for a while and stared into space, then, as if deciding, picked up her mobile phone and dialled a number.

'Magda, it's me,' she said into the mouthpiece.

A sing-song voice answered.

'Don't tell me you're cancelling tonight; I'm rather looking forward to seeing that film.'

'No, I'm not,' Gerry replied. 'I need to ask you something.'
'Shoot.'

'It's about one of my pupils, Toby Anson, who used to be in your reception class.'

'Oh, yes, Toby, the sweetest boy,' Magda said; she sounded to Gerry as if she were smiling. 'You're getting your schoolwork out of the way as usual. Why, what's wrong with Toby?'

'Nothing, I mean, uhh,' she sighed. 'Do you remember what his performance was like? His reading, writing and grasp of maths?'

Magda was quiet for a few seconds. 'Yes, I do,' she said, 'he was behind his peers and was average in his baseline assessment. I didn't want to...you know, make too much of it—some are slower at first, but they catch up.'

'How long should one wait, though? I want all my students to pass the phonics test at the end of the year. Don't you think it's wise to deal with the issue sooner rather than later?'

'That depends on what the issue is. Is Toby not showing any signs of improvement then?' Magda asked.

'Not really. I'm pulling together reports for the national curriculum assessments on Monday, and I know what they will say about him. I feel he needs some one-on-one attention and tutoring, and I might be able to work closely with him and, you know, find out the root cause – there's always something. I can tell that he has a lot to say; he's quite vocal at the best of times and is quite a brilliant child, and I want to help.'

'Wait until Monday then, and then we can take it from there, OK? See you tonight.'

***

'I do know what I'm saying, Mrs Lawson; I have helped so many pupils in the past who were diagnosed with dyslexia. I'm not saying that he is, but at least let me try working with him out of school hours and in my own time and then perform an assessment; if that doesn't work, then you can give the approval for him to undertake a dyslexia assessment with the special needs coordinator.' Gerry fixed the headmistress with a steady gaze.

'This is very unorthodox, Mrs Lawson; I cannot believe you would even entertain such a request from one of your staff – it's too informal.'

Gerry and Mrs Lawson looked at the head of the curriculum assessment board who had spoken.

'For your information, Mr Kapler, Miss Bray has been teaching for over eight years and has come to this school highly recommended. As you put it, I welcome "staff" like her and will allow her to give extra assistance to this child. I trust her judgment.' Mrs Lawson adjusted her pince-nez and looked at Gerry. Her eyes, Gerry thought, always looked twice their size through the spectacles.

'Miss Bray, this is for a very short time, and you must report progress to me fortnightly. It's unusual for me to take this course of action, but,' she flung her hand in the air, 'what the heck?'

There was a collective gasp from the two curriculum assessors.

'This is my school!' Mrs Lawson finished.

***

'So, are you saying he needs extra lessons?' Joel Anson stood outside the school entrance with Gerry.

'Yes, but you don't need to worry about extra costs,' Gerry said. 'I am happy just to do it.'

She looked at Joel. His face showed the beginnings of stubble, and he kept running his fingers through his wavy hair as he turned to look at his son, who was playing games on his phone. His dark brown hair, the same colour as his son's, fell forward onto his forehead in the same way and needed a cut, she noticed again.

She realised she hadn't taken a good look at him the first time they had met, and on subsequent occasions, she had only seen him at a distance in the car park. He was around five feet ten inches tall and wore light blue jeans and a well-fitted plain white T-shirt that showed off a slim, muscular physique. His eyes were dark hazel, his nose slightly wide, and his generous mouth downturned at the corners.

'So,' he said again as if trying to get his head around the topic, 'are you going to teach him here after school hours, my house or your house?'

'Wherever is comfortable for him: my house to start, you could arrange for him to be picked up,' Gerry replied.

'No, I always do that myself.'

His eyes seemed to her to be moving over her face, taking in her softly packed afro hair and mocha-coloured skin.

She yawned. 'Oh, I'm sorry. It has nothing to do with you,' she said as he began to smile. 'I've been in a couple of meetings today and am a bit tired.'

She smoothed her dress down as he continued to look at her. Not feeling her best bothered her, and she didn't know why.

Not knowing what to do, she smiled, her well-shaped lips, devoid of lipstick, curved upwards.

'Well, bring Toby tomorrow after he has rested around five,' she said, handing him her address. 'We'll take it from there.'

He nodded, 'Thank you for doing this. I appreciate it.'

She waved his words away and said goodbye to Toby.

***

'Do you want some more lemonade, Toby?' Gerry asked, holding the bottle.

'No, thank you, Miss, my belly's sticking out,' he paused, lowering his voice as if letting her into a secret. 'Grandma's making dinner tonight: chicken nuggets and chips, my favourite,' he finished with a flourish.

They both laughed.

'Does Grandma live with you?' Gerry asked.

'Not really, but she comes to care for me,' he replied.

She thought he sounded a tad too severe for a boy his age.

'She has never come to pick you up, though?' Gerry ventured, wanting to know more about the Anson household.

'No, only daddy does that,' he said, matter-of-fact.

'Well, let's finish our lesson; you're doing very well, Toby.' She watched the smile spread across his face.

***

Two days later, Gerry looked at the clock, frowning as there was no sign of Toby and Joel.

She stood looking out of the living room window onto the drive as it was getting late, expecting to see Joel's Volkswagen Golf turning in. She thought about phoning Magda but decided against it as Magda had been teasing her about Joel,

"I think he's gorgeous," she said to Gerry. "What are you waiting for, girl? Toby loves you; that has got to be a good starting point."

Gerry didn't want to dwell on Magda's comments at all; there was no doubt that she felt something for Joel, but her priority was Toby, and besides, she knew nothing about Joel. She felt something wasn't quite right; something was missing, but she didn't quite know what.

She picked up the phone and dialled.

'Hi Joel, this is Gerry; why haven't you brought Toby over?' she asked.

'Why?' he repeated her question back to her. 'Because I don't like my son being interrogated. I appreciate you helping him, but if you wanted inside information on my family or our arrangements, you should have asked me and not tried to squeeze it out of a vulnerable little boy,' he replied, all in one breath.

Gerry caught her breath, her left hand holding her forehead as she tried to steady her right hand; the phone rattled against her ear.

'I'm afraid you've got things wrong,' Gerry's voice broke. 'We were having a conversation. As you put it, I didn't squeeze any information out of him. Toby was speaking as kids do, and yes, I asked him a question, but...' she paused, 'I was certainly not interrogating him. I would never do that.'

'You didn't coerce him into divulging information?' he asked accusingly.

'Maybe...maybe, I said something, but I didn't ask him direct questions or coerce him.' She let out her breath, unsure of what to say next. 'Look, I'm sorry. I have offended you, but that doesn't mean you should stop his extra lessons. Why don't I come to your place, and you can supervise both of us from now on, starting today?'

He was quiet for a while. 'OK. I'll text our address,' he said quietly.

'Thanks,' she said, relieved.

'See you later.'

***

'I'm sorry for how I spoke to you on the phone,' Joel said as they sat in his living room. 'I wanted to ease my conscience, so I asked you to come. I knew Toby would already be in bed; he said he was tired. It was his sports day, well, of course, you would know.'

'He's doing very well. I'm quite amazed at his progress,' Gerry said, 'and there's also no need to apologise; I would expect any responsible parent to have behaved similarly.'

'Thank you for being so considerate,' he said, smiling. 'Can I get you a drink: tea, coffee?'

'Tea would be nice, thank you.'

She took the opportunity to look around. She had expected a small bachelor pad since neither mentioned a wife or mother, and he didn't wear a wedding ring, but the house had a warm family feel. She thought it was very comfortable, well decorated, and well taken care of—it must be the grandmother. It was a large house, big enough for a family of five plus pets.

Joel put the tea down, sat beside her on the soft, brown couch and surprised her with what he said next.

'My wife left me three years ago when Toby was two. She didn't just get up and go; she was one of those free-spirited people, and I knew that from the beginning of our relationship. I just hoped she would settle, that her insatiable thirst for travelling would gradually diminish – it did for a while.' He paused and looked at her. 'I mean, she stopped travelling and stayed put for a while. When Toby was born, I thought that was it; she wasn't going anywhere, but I could sense something boiling beneath the surface; she was never really comfortable with family life. She went on two short holidays, saying she needed to get away, and then one day, she just took off, permanently.'

'Are you in contact with her?' Gerry asked.

'For the first eighteen months, I was. I tried to lure her back; I sent her photos and videos of Toby changing from baby to infant, birthdays, and first day in reception and school, but it didn't work; she was in South America and on the move.'

He shifted his seating position. 'Everybody said she would return, but I think they all changed their minds after a year.'

'Does Toby know what happened?'

'No, surprisingly, he doesn't ask many questions either. I believe this problem in school stemmed from an emotional depth of confusion, you know, him keeping everything inside about his mother. I see you thought so, too,' he said as she nodded.

'He's swift to hold my hand and is very affectionate towards me in my home,' Gerry said, 'but very controlled at school. Since he started coming to my place, it's as if his work has deliberately improved.' She paused, 'I don't know if he told you, but we play games as well; he's a very loving child and needs to be—'

'I do love him, his Nana, and I take good care of him. I spend most of my time working from home, so I'm always here for him.' He added sheepishly, 'It helps that I own the firm, but I honestly couldn't do any more.'

'I understand, and I think you're doing fine. I feel that Toby's keeping it all in because he isn't asking questions. He sees the other mothers waiting at the gate for his friends; he's scared to ask for his, scared of the answer. Maybe he feels she will turn up one day if he doesn't ask. Speak to him a bit more, open up to him.'

They both heard a cough near the door.

'Mum, this is Gerry, Toby's tutor. Gerry, this is Pat.'

'It's nice to meet you, Pat,' Gerry smiled, but she only received a mumbled reply as she turned and walked away.

Joel coughed and looked down at the floor.

Gerry picked up her bag and car keys. 'I better be going. I've got to meet someone.'

'A date?' he asked, 'standing up. 'Oh, I'm sorry. It's none of my business.'

'No, not a date,' she replied, looking at him as he looked away. 'You know Magda from school?'

He nodded.

'We're going out for a meal with some other friends – it's her birthday.'

As she got into her Audi, Joel closed the car door for her, not saying anything.

She sat there trying to think of something to say, afraid that if she started the engine, it might drown out her words.

'I was wondering,' Joel started and then coughed. 'I was wondering whether I could take you out maybe at the weekend for a meal.' He now looked Gerry straight in the eye.

She hesitated for a while. 'Yes, that would be nice.'

Joel smiled fully for the first time since she had met him, and his whole face lit up; she could not help but return it.

'See you on Saturday then,' he said, still smiling.

As she pulled away, she noticed the twitching curtains upstairs.

***

'Miss, Miss, are you okay?' A tiny voice chirped. 'Are you daydreaming?'

Gerry blinked and looked straight into Lucy's freckled face. Lucy's head was bent sideways, looking into Gerry's face, her big blonde curls dangling; the whole class giggled.

'All right, guys, all right. It's time for PE,' Gerry shouted.

They let out a squeal of delight.

Dinner with Joel on Saturday was fantastic; they talked on the phone after she returned from church all day on Sunday. They were seeing each other tonight when he brought Toby over.

***

Gerry hadn't heard from Joel and Toby in three days—it was mid-term, and she knew they hadn't planned to travel. She wanted to call but thought it might be too forward, and she couldn't find an excuse to see Toby either, as she only gave extra lessons during term time.

She paced up and down her living room floor and eventually decided to do some gardening. She was taking her tools out of the shed when her phone rang. She realised later that she had never run so fast in her life.

'Gerry, it's me,' Joel said. 'I'm sorry for not calling, but Toby and I have had to sort some things out; we're by the beach in Brighton.'

'What do you mean?' her heart skipped a beat. 'Is something wrong with him?'

'No,' she sensed that he was hesitating. 'His mother came back three days ago.'

Gerry felt a thud in her chest. Holding the phone, her right hand started to shake so much that she had to transfer it to her left.

'And...' she prompted.

'We went away to talk; it appears he knew all along about her and the situation; his Nana had let it slip in her conversations. Toby didn't show any bonding or affection for his mother whatsoever.'

'Well, I'm not surprised,' Gerry said. 'How is he?'

'Fine, he's much stronger, less shy. He told Leanne that he wanted a proper mummy who would always be there for him and not one who was always on holiday - he said it to her face.'

Gerry could hardly contain her relief; she knew it was selfish, but still, yet...

'So, what happens now?' she asked.

'We'll be on our way back to London soon. I mean, Toby and I. Leanne's on her way to Dover; she's catching the Sea ferry to France; she'll keep in contact more often, she promises. We'll have to see how it goes.' He paused for a few seconds. 'Can we come to your place on our way back? Toby has been asking for you, and I...well, I'd like to see you too.'

Gerry began to relax for the first time since the beginning of the conversation.

'Of course, of course you can,' she repeated, 'I'll be waiting.'

***

'Do you think your mother is afraid of another woman taking over?' They talked at her kitchen table while Toby watched the television in the living room.

'She's not my mother, she's—oh, you thought...no, no,' he waved his hand. 'She's Leanne's mother, my mother-in-law. She moved in for a while after Leanne left, but now she comes three times a week because I'm around most of the time. I'm quite fond of her, so I call her Mum.'

He looked down at his hand, continuing.

'I spoke to her yesterday; she knows deep down inside that her daughter isn't coming back, and she blames herself for not being firm enough with her when raising her. Her husband died, and she brought Leanne up as a single mother.' He paused. 'Leanne told her three days ago that she wasn't returning, and even if she did, it wouldn't be to us. I have moved on, and I want Toby to as well. Leanne has accepted that and that I will also remarry someday.'

He looked into Gerry's face and quickly changed the subject.

She thought it was because he was unsure of what her response would be.

'The report from school was fantastic. I'm so proud of Toby,' Joel said, 'and thankful to you.'

They looked into each other's eyes across the table for a while, his hands holding hers.

'What's wrong?' They hadn't noticed Toby had come in.

'Nothing,' they said together and laughed.

'What's funny?' he asked.

'Nothing,' they said again. They continued to laugh, and Toby joined them.

'Older people are strange; they talk funny,' Toby said as his dad pulled him onto his lap.

'You did so well in school, son,' he ruffled his hair. 'I'm so proud of you. How about we get something to eat and take Gerry with us?'

'That will be great, Dad. Miss Bray is lovely, and I like her a lot,' he said, smiling at Gerry with that gap between his teeth that made her heart melt so...

'So do I, son, and we'll be seeing a lot more of each other from now on. What do you think about that?' Joel asked Toby.

'Fantastic,' he said with glee. He jumped off his dad's lap and ran towards the hallway to get his coat. 'Last one out is a wobblemonger.'

'A what?' Joel looked at Gerry, perplexed.

'Don't ask. It's one of the words I use when telling stories, and it keeps them attentive. It's a long word, too.'

He pulled her closer and kissed her.

'It is indeed Miss Bray. '

The End.

8. ABI

Abi opened her front door.

'Oh, hi, Mum?'

'Hello Love. How was work?' Her mother asked.

'OK. The London Underground must be the hottest in the world – I could hardly breathe.' She kissed her mother on both cheeks. 'I wasn't expecting you until 8 pm. Is everything okay?'

'Yes dear, I just thought I'd leave home early because of the rush hour traffic,' she replied.

'Go on, Mum, something's on your mind?'

She shook her head. 'Nothing, darling'

'OK, I know you, Mum, but it can wait.' She smiled at her mother. Time had been kind to her, Abi thought as she walked towards her room; it was as if she were looking at a reflection of herself – the oblong-shaped face, the large dark round eyes, the slightly rounded nose, and the full lips, even their facial expressions, people often remarked, were the same.

Abi's mother spoke fast. 'Abi, your father wants to come and visit from abroad; he wants to come and see you and your sister and brothers.'

'What?' Abi turned around. 'You know how it is with him.' She covered her eyes with her hand. 'He can visit those *other* people, his other family. I want nothing to do with him.'

Her mother winced as the door slammed shut.

A few moments later, Abi returned wearing jeans and a tee shirt. Standing with her back to her mother, she tapped an app on her phone, and an Ella Fitzgerald song started playing on her Bose system. 'What would you like for dinner?' she asked without turning around.

With a tired sigh, she turned and looked around the room – everywhere but at her mother.

This was her favourite room. She had chosen contemporary dark oak furniture, a low centre table, and a bookcase to contrast the intense yellow shade on the walls, curtains, and rugs. A tall glass cabinet in the corner was filled with pottery and porcelain sculptures from her travels.

The bookcase held her music collection, books on African art, and photographs of her mother, two brothers, and her sister.

Her mother spoke first, 'Abi, I know it's hard to forgive him—'

Abi shook her head, 'No, you don't understand. Mum, I have forgiven him; he's not worth that much time or energy.' She took a deep breath, 'Look, Mum, Dana and the twins are well taken care of,' she leaned forward, 'we don't need him back in our lives.'

'He's still your father no matter what,' she pleaded. 'I know he didn't take care of all of you as he should have, but—'

'That's an understatement,' Abi shouted. 'Have you forgotten how he ruined your life? Do I need to spell it out, Mum? How is it possible to have two families simultaneously in the same city? He was leading a double life, and life is about making choices—he made his. We were starved, mum, of affection, attention, everything.' She sat down. 'He is never,

never stepping foot in this house. If his other, other... whatever they are to him, want to help him, that's their business, but I know they won't.'

'How do you know that?' Her mother's voice broke as she dabbed away tears with a tissue.

'I just do, Mum. He probably wants us to pay his airfare as well.' Her mother looked away. 'Yes, I'm not surprised. He sees you as a soft touch, you know.'

'He doesn't. I'm just trying to get you to understand ... to understand...you're my eldest; if you forgive, the others will follow,' she implored. 'All I want is peace.'

'I want peace too, mum. We have a new life, and he's not welcome.' She gently cupped her mother's cheek in her right hand and kissed her forehead. 'You have shed enough tears—no more.' Abi kissed her forehead again.

She turned and walked towards the kitchen. 'How does rice, spinach, and grilled goat meat sound?'

***

Four months later.

'That's enough boys. Come and sit at the table,' Abi's mum said to the twins. 'Dana, please help.' She sighed aloud.

Si held Jay in a mock headlock, both boys panting with exhaustion.

'Ouch,' Jay screamed.

'Thirteen-year-olds behaving like kids. Sit down.' Dana said, holding them apart. 'I said sit down at the table.'

Abi laughed, looking at her younger sister, a taller version of herself.

'That boxing you do has paid off; it's a good thing, is, that you have strong arms.'

Dana nodded.

'With these two,' she pushed them gently into their chairs and took hers, it certainly is.'

Abi looked at her mum, smiling, 'Mum, say grace, please.'

They sat around a large ornate birch dining table, which took centre stage in a large, airy, bright, yellow kitchen, a shade lighter than the living room.

'Dig in,' Abi said after her mother had said grace. They passed the food round.

'Yum,' Jay said, all my favourites at once: boiled yam, spinach, and chargrilled beef in pepper sauce.'

They all laughed.

'So, what's new?' Abi spoke with a mouthful of yam and spinach.

'Nothing much,' Dana replied. 'It's been a busy week: meetings, client parties after work, and then dad's documents took up a lot of my time—'

Abi's head shot up. 'What did you say?'

Dana stared at her plate, cutting her food into small portions but not eating.

'Abi, I asked Dana to send the documents that your father required to get a visa,' her mother spoke in an undertone. 'I—'

Abi gesticulated. 'Mum, please let Dana speak.' She focused her gaze on Dana. 'She's got a lot to say at the best of times and is never lost for words.'

Dana looked away, almost whispering. 'Mum asked me to send him the documents.'

The tinkling sound of cutlery against plates stopped.

'She had to, Abi,' Si said tearfully. 'We had to help Dad.'

'Have you forgotten the pain we all went through, Dana? How emotionally bereft we were when Dad left? How we struggled as a family to get back on our feet, picking up the remnants? Is your memory so fleeting?' She knocked the table with her knuckle.

Abi pushed her chair back and folded her arms. She pressed her lips together, looking from one to the other as if resigned. 'I seem to be the only one in the dark here,' she said quietly.

'No,' her mother began tearfully. 'You're not.'

'Is there anything else? I mean, I trust you guys,' she swallowed. 'What else are you holding back from me?'

The boys looked down at their plates, her mother looked at Dana, and Dana stared at the door.

Abi bent her head, rubbing her forehead as if trying to erase tension.

'Abi,' Dana's voice shook. 'You weren't supposed to find out this way; we were going to tell you after lunch.'

'How long have you been in contact with him?' she asked without looking up.

'About four months,' Si mumbled after a short silence.

Abi let out a deep breath. 'Finish your lunch,' she said.

She wiped her mouth with the napkin, threw it on the table, and walked out, leaving the sound of the door reverberating in her wake.

***

Abi sat on the park bench. She loved summer; the grass was a soft, lush green carpet, and the lilies and scented roses were in full bloom. The warm, moist air was heavy, like an invisible blanket. It was quiet, save for the chirps of the birds and their young.

Her ringtone broke the silence.

'Hello?'

'Hi, sweetheart.'

'Hi, Mum,' she replied.

'Where are you? I rang you earlier, sweetheart; you're usually home by now. Are you in the park again, alone?'

'I'm fine,' she replied. 'It's just getting dark now, so I'll be heading off soon.'

'We need to talk. You've been so distant since the luncheon. I'm worried.'

'There's no need to be mum,' she said. 'I'm fine.'

'Please, Abi, I know you're hurting. I love you so much, sweetheart. I want to come and see you. Please let's talk this through,' her mum's voice pleaded.

'Mum, I'll call you later.'

She switched off her mobile and rested her head on her lap. A few minutes later, she began to sob, at first quietly and then louder.

Abi didn't care who saw her.

***

The leaves were turning brown and deep red, the summer temperatures were dipping fast, and the wind grew stronger and bolder.

Abi drew in a deep breath. There was something about this time of year, with old things dying and the expectation of the new. She walked down her mother's street, smiling as the leaves fell from the trees, coaxed by the wind.

Abi pressed her mother's doorbell.

The large door swung open.

'Hello, Sweetheart,' her mum kissed both Abi's cheeks. 'My goodness, have you lost weight?'

'Hi, Mum,' she stepped through the door. 'Just a little; it's been manic at work.'

'Oh, sweetheart, they do work you too hard.'

Abi followed her mum into the Living room. It was filled with soft furnishings in brown and tawny gold. She stopped in her tracks.

'Hello Abi, my dear, it's been a long time.'

Abi stared.

'Will you not return my embrace?'

'Sit down dear,' her mother pointed to the seat beside the man who had spoken when Abi neither replied nor responded.

Abi took the seat opposite instead. She sat staring at a daytime soap on the TV.

'I arrived yesterday, Abi; your mother didn't mention it to you on the phone this morning; she wasn't sure you would come.'

'Maybe she was right,' she replied slowly, looking at her mother, who looked away.

'Would you like some lunch, dear?' Abi's mum addressed her.

'No, thank you,' Abi replied stoically.

'I will get you a drink.' Abi's mother broke the silence and left the room.

Her father coughed twice. 'Abi, we have a lot to talk about.'

Abi looked at her father; his long legs were stretched out in front of him; he was over six feet tall. She hadn't seen him in seven years, and she stared at him; his dark complexion, his hair; short, black, and curly; his close-cut beard, now completely grey; the lines on his forehead were deep, and his eyes, eyes she remembered used to smile into hers as she laughed when he tickled her mercilessly as a child, now seemed dull, as if time had diminished the light in them.

'You observe me as a stranger would, Abi,' he said quietly.

Abi looked away, 'You want to talk; I'm listening. I don't have a choice,' she continued under her breath.

Her mother returned and placed a drink on a side table.

'Thank you,' Abi said without making eye contact.

'Abi,' her father spoke. 'I have come because I want reconciliation. I'm sorry for all the pain I've caused. I'm trying to turn things around, change this situation.'

'What things?' Abi asked, staring at him.

'The way we are—I mean as a family,' he replied in a warm, timbre tone.

'Oh, but you can't just magic things away: pain, rejection, hurt,' she said breathlessly. 'It's not possible. "The situation", as you put it, is too far gone - irreversible. Even we,' she pointed to her mother, 'are split because of you.'

'I want my family to move forward, Abi, not backwards. I can't change the past, but I want to be here for you all from here onwards,'

She pursed her lips. 'That sounds excellent, it does, but there's a small problem, you see – we've come a long way since we left you, Dad; I meant since *you* left us, and we've moved on.'

She stared at the TV, the room silent except for her agitated breathing. She turned back to him.

'How's your family?' Abi asked. 'You haven't mentioned them–not once.'

He looked away. 'Don't sound so sarcastic. You're still my child.'

'How come you're not with them?' she continued, ignoring him. 'Have you abandoned them to defect back to us?' She leaned forward in her seat. 'The others seem to have been seduced by your charms. I haven't.'

She stood up suddenly, ignoring her mother's arm that had reached out to hold her.

She looked him straight in the eye.

'Go back to your *family*, Dad.' She wiped the tears running down her face with the back of her hand. 'Remember, your old tricks – here one minute—'

'Listen, Abi, please,' he stood up. 'I do love you and have never stopped caring.' He raised his hand as she was about to speak. 'No, please let me finish. I made mistakes that I am not proud of.'

Abi turned and walked to the front window, arms folded across her chest.

'Excuses, excuses, it won't make the hurt disappear, Dad. Can I still call you that?' She turned and looked at him, 'It's just that...it seems so strange after all this time.'

Her mother began to cry.

'See,' Abi said, looking at her father. 'You've brought her nothing but pain and misery.'

'Abi, I'm trying—'

'You can't try hard enough, so don't bother.' She snatched her bag up.

'Your brothers and sister think differently. Why can't you forgive me?' He implored her.

'They don't see you for who you are; they don't know you.'

'Who am I, Abi, who?' His voice rose. 'You think you know me, but you don't.'

Abi raised her hands as if in defeat and moved towards the door. 'I don't want to and don't need to hear this.' She suddenly stopped and spun around on her heels, returning to him.

They stood silently, facing each other.

Her mother's sobbing grew louder, breaking the silence. They both ignored her.

He reached out to touch her arm.

'Abi, you're my firstborn, and I love you,' he spoke softly, 'I don't want to go on like this anymore,' he pleaded as he moved closer to her. 'There is so much you don't know, so much.'

'Stop it, please.' She covered her ears, the veins in her neck standing out.

'I am trying to explain, but you—' he raised his voice.

'Stop it, Stop it! Both of you.'

They both turned.

'I can't take this anymore,' her mother said, looking at her husband. 'I'm sorry, Patrick.'

'No,' he said, 'don't...don't say anything.'

'I'm sorry, this has to stop,' she stepped away, avoiding his outstretched hand.

'Abi, look at me,' her mother wiped her tears with the palm of her hand. 'It's my fault, everything. Think back. You were old enough. When did things start going wrong? Think.'

Abi stood looking at her mother, her forehead furrowing in a frown, her hands at her side.

'Think back,' her mother repeated. 'It was just before the twins were born. Do you remember now? You were twelve then and started asking why Daddy wasn't at home. The answer to that, Abi, is...' she paused, her eyes filled with tears spilling down her cheeks, 'the twins, your baby brothers,' she paused again and took a deep breath, 'they are not your father's.' She looked down at the carpet, 'I was lonely; it's not an excuse, but things weren't going well between us; your dad was travelling a lot...and I had an affair.' She looked at Abi. 'You remember him, don't you? Yes, I can see you do.'

Abi stared at her mother; she dropped her bag, covered her mouth, and sat down on the long settee with a thump. Her parents stood looking down at her. Head in hand, she began to cry, with sobs racking her body.

'Mum, say it's not true. Why? Why?'

Her father sat beside her, touching her shoulder.

'Abi, I would never have told you.' He sighed, 'I lost the will to live when I found out that your mother was pregnant by someone else because I loved her so much. I felt rejected and betrayed, and though I forgave her and stayed until Si and Jay started school, I went looking for love elsewhere. I found solace in my new family when Ola got pregnant. It was the biggest mistake of my life; I should have stayed or at least worked something out for you and Dana's sake. The twins and Dana don't know anything about this, and I want it to stay that way—at least for now. Let's start afresh as a family; we have a lot of time to make up for.' He squeezed her fingers gently in his hands. 'Remember how it used to be? What do you say?'

Abi looked at her mum and then her dad.

'I wish it were that easy,' she replied. 'Mum, please stop crying.'

'I know it's not all going to fall back into place, but at least, let's start somewhere, huh? What do you say? Take each day at a time.' Her father said. 'Abi, look at me.'

'I don't know; this family has too many lies. I can't, I can't comprehend all this; it's too much. Mum, please stop crying.'

'I wanted to tell you, but you were so bitter, and I didn't want that bitterness directed at me. Forgive me, Abi,' her mum said.

Abi stood and wiped her mum's tears, hugging her.

'We'll get through this. Somehow.'

'Abi, let's start afresh,' her father reached out, touching her shoulder.

Abi turned to him. 'There is the matter of your, uh... what happens now?'

'Ola has moved on, but I still see my son. I won't shirk my responsibilities.' He looked at her and then away. 'Perhaps one day you'll meet him.'

'Perhaps,' Abi said with a watery smile. 'Yes...sure.'

'Oh, Abi,' her mum hugged her tightly.

Abi raised her hand, looking from one to the other and smiling.

'One day at a time.'

The End.

Abi. © Kemi Kotun

9. TOMORROW'S BEGINNINGS

'Mum, I have to go for this interview. This is the seventh one in three months that I have turned down because—'

'Because your mother is ill,' Irene Cantrell shouted at her daughter, her dark eyes blazing. 'Remember your priorities, young woman. 'I am your mother,' she ended up almost on a scream.

Landa Hayes sat cross-legged on the window seat, looking out onto the bleak street as she had since childhood. Bleak like her life was now. She couldn't see beyond the buildings on the other side: the Conway, the Walter and the Ahmad families–and that's how she felt, blocked in. At least as a child, she could go out and play, if only with Melanie, her Irish neighbour next door—the only neighbours her mother got along with.

Now, at twenty-four years old, she felt left behind. Melanie had long left home, first to go to university and then to get a job in the City of London, as had the rest of her classmates on her street.

She sighed, holding her head in her arms.

'I don't know how long I can last,' she whispered.

'Huh? Did you say something, Landa?'

She looked at her mother and shook her head.

'No, mother, I didn't.'

She rose slowly as if her bones were aching and walked towards the door, stopping only to look down at her dishevelled mother.

Irene Cantrell sat in the corner of the soft blue sofa. Her once lovely, thick dark hair was now grey and unkempt. Her silky skin, always smooth and clear, was now lined with deep grooves, making her look like the wind-whipped trunk of an aged tree. Her legs hung over the edge, covered in thick, long socks, which began where her knee-length floral dress ended.

Landa looked into her mother's eyes, and that feeling of despair flooded her chest in a rush—that same feeling she experienced as a child when she knew her presence alone couldn't keep her dad with them – her fears had given way to reality. She hoped this wouldn't end the same way.

'I'll put dinner on,' Landa said, opening the door.

'Landa...' her mum said, her voice pleading, 'don't go away and leave me.'

Her gloomy smile reflected her thoughts. 'Don't worry, Mum, I'm here for you.'

***

Landa sat in her aunt's sitting room.

'This is the only place in the world that I feel happy, Aunty Jos, sitting here looking at all these artefacts you've collected on your travels.' She shook her head, 'It makes me feel that while I've lost hope—'

'Landa, look at me. You'll always have hope as long as I'm alive and even after I'm gone.' Aunt Jos' strong voice boomed. She raised her hand as Landa was about to speak. 'I know what you're going to say; I know there's a situation here that we need to deal with, but something's got to give, and it will.'

'I don't think you understand, Aunty Jos; she's not getting any better. Mum's totally reliant on me for everything. I've no job, no qualifications except for my business diploma, and I'm not even interested in business. You know, I wanted to follow in your footsteps and study archaeology; it's always been my passion.'

Aunty Jos was nodding. Her kind eyes looked directly at her niece.

'I know I've said this a hundred times, Landa, but I told your father to stay.'

'He couldn't Aunty Jos.'

'I know you'll always defend him, but I reminded him that our mother stayed because of us; she didn't run away and leave us although she had every reason to; your grandfather was a dunk and a... a wife beater.'

'I know,' she looked at her aunt, tears welling in her eyes.

'Aww, come here.' She pulled Landa into an embrace and held her there. 'I feel we've failed you, Landa, your dad, your mum and I. You were always a bright child, always first in class, and ambitious—and look at you at twenty-four, a full-time carer for a mother who *isn't* sick.'

Landa pulled out of her aunt's arms. 'She is tough, Aunty Jos.'

Aunty Jos shook her head.

'She's not. She's afraid of being alone. Her sisters stopped speaking to her, her husband left her, she stopped working, and it's all on you.' She raised Landa's chin with her hand, looking at her face. 'You're strong. Strong, like my mother was, bringing up six of us while dad frittered what little earnings he made on the horses. And you're beautiful; your thick, lovely black hair, honey-coloured eyes and gorgeous olive skin – I must say that was from your mother.'

She laughed. 'That's the first time I've ever heard you credit something good to her, Aunty Jos. I'm proud to be part Jamaican and a quarter Spanish.'

'You're three-quarters Jamaican; don't leave out your feisty grandma; perhaps that's why your mother is hanging onto you; your grandmother was too hard on her.' She sighed, getting up and pulling her towards the kitchen. 'I can't stand by and let her ruin your life. I can't pretend it will end tomorrow, the next day, and the next year. That's like a longing that makes you sick because it never happens.' She turned, holding Landa's shoulders. 'Landa, I'm going to call your father. Something needs to be done.'

***

'I've got tickets, Landa. It's a day trip; you can't be chained to Aylesbury all year.' Chris stopped her hand as she went to turn on the tap, 'Leave the coffee; in fact, why don't we go out to Costa; we can sit and chat...' he looked towards the slightly open door leading to the corridor, 'in private.'

Landa shook her head and turned, and he grabbed and kissed her. 'Let's go. I'll bring you back in an hour—you haven't been in my new car yet,' he beamed, 'and I've had it for three months.'

Landa smiled back.

'You know,' she whispered, 'I live for these visits.' She locked her fingers over his low-cut nape, his afro hair springy under her fingers – she remembered when they had first met that she'd called him sponge-head because of his curly hair. 'I need this respite, Chris, but I can't leave her alone.'

He kissed her high cheekbone and whispered, 'Yes, you can. Come with me, Landa; I want to spend some time with you, not whisk you away forever–as much as I'd love to.'

'OK. Let me see if she's all right, then we can go.'

He held her, his strong arms locked around her waist as he pulled her close, kissing her.

She tore from Chris' arms and ran towards the kitchen door without looking at him as she heard her mother scream.

'Landa, Landa, help me...I've fallen off the sofa.'

'Mum.' She flung open the sitting room door and dashed across the small expanse of floor, bending to place her hand under her mother's head as she lay on the floor.

'What happened?' Landa asked breathlessly, her palm flat on her chest. 'Did you hit your head, Mum?'

'I think so, Landa. I tried to reach the remote control to switch on the TV, but you left it too far away.' She looked at her with an accusatory stare.

'I didn't mum. I left it on the side table right beside you this morning. How did it get onto the centre table? You must have placed it there. Mum, you have to help me get you up. You're not injured,' she said, wiping her forehead as beads of sweat appeared.

'How can you say that, Landa?' her mother's mouth twisted.' You're being horrid to me.'

'Mum, please...'

'Just lift me.'

'Mum, you know you can walk; your physiotherapist said you can, and I know you can. You need to work those muscles.'

'I am. I mean, I will, but I need you, Landa,' tears rolled down her face. 'You know I'm not usually like this, but I just need to return to normal.'

The front doorbell rang.

'Who's that?'

'It must be Aunty Jos; she said she would pop around.'

'What for?' she asked. Her expression changed to anger. 'What does she want? I don't want anything to do with your father's family.' She shouted. 'Nothing,'

Landa silently straightened her mother's hair and brushed it back.

'It's too late; Chris has already let her in.' She sat beside her mother. 'Mum, she's my blood; please be civil to her.'

She arranged the blanket Landa gave her over her knees. 'I don't know why he's letting people into someone else's house. That's just bad manners,' she retorted.

'Come on, Mum, you know he knows Aunty Jos quite well – she's no stranger to him.'

Her mother hissed in response.

Landa moved towards the door, wanting to escape the horrid atmosphere. The tension made her head ache, and she knew it would only worsen when Aunty Jos entered. She literally ran through the door, bumping into her aunt.

'Landa honey, what's the rush?'

She kissed both her cheeks and stepped back.

'Come.' Aunty Jos took her hand, leading her to the kitchen. 'Chris is taking you out; we've just discussed,' she stopped and looked at him, and he nodded. 'Go and enjoy yourself while I speak to your mother.' She let go of her hand and walked away. 'Oh, by the way, where is the letter you received confirming the interview you missed.'

'It's on the table in the sitting room, Aunty Jos.'

'OK, dear. Go with Chris now. I'm expecting someone to join us.' She winked.'

Landa's face lit up.

'Go,' her aunt said again and closed the door.

***

Landa and Chris sipped cappuccinos in Costa.

Chris took her hand across the table and held it. 'I wonder what your aunt...and your dad are saying.'

She shook her head. 'I don't want to think about it.'

He sat looking at her for a while.

'What, Chris? Why are you looking at me like that?'

'You're the victim here, Landa. You're the one that fell between the cracks of your parent's marriage. When your dad couldn't take your mother's controlling ways anymore, he took off – leaving you as a twelve-year-old.'

'They were unhappy, Dad wanted to stay, and after all these years, he still thinks there's a chance they will reconcile; that's how deep their love was, but Mum is hard and unforgiving.'

'I thought she was the problem.'

'Not to start with. Dad had an affair, a short one which he broke off before it even started; they never recovered, no matter how much he repented and tried to make it right. Mum was enraged, and I would listen late at night when she would verbally abuse him.' She looked at him with tears in her eyes.

Chris squeezed her hand. 'It's all right, Landa. It's going to be fine from here on.'

'I tried to make up for what Dad did—'

'You can't do that, Landa. You can't take responsibility for someone else's mistake and try to rectify it; that's why you're so emotionally drained.'

She shook her head. 'Chris, you don't understand. I wanted the beautiful days back again, the way we were before. The holidays, Christmas morning, my birthday parties and their birthdays.'

Chris dabbed a tear from her cheek.

She continued, 'I thought I could make things right, but it took a twist – mum fell ill when I was sixteen while studying for my 'O' Levels, and that was the start.'

'But she got better and returned to work?'

'Yes, but she'd lost something; that strong woman I'd always known just disappeared. It was as if she gave up.'

'And you took over?'

She nodded, looking down at the table. 'I got admission to university to study archaeology, but she became housebound and wouldn't leave her room. She said she couldn't bear to live if I left.'

'Look at me, Landa, you can't live your life for your mother or anybody else. You're being emotionally blackmailed, and everyone can see it but you because, in your mind, you're trying to right something that's not your responsibility.' His voice softened. 'Let's take small steps. We'll go to the concert in London, visit Melanie, and catch a few events this week. We'll do something different next week, whatever gets you out of the house.'

With a faint smile, she said, 'I know what you're thinking—that Mum will become more independent in my absence.'

'Yes—because she can.'

She squeezed his hand. 'You know how much I love you, Chris?'

'Yes. You're special, Landa, and smart – you don't want to throw away this time in your life and become bitter about it later – nip it before it grows.'

'I believe Dad's joined Aunty Jos at the house now.'

Chris nodded. 'She said he would. She is a tough one – your aunt.'

'Yes, but so is my mother; she'll find that strength again; I know she will.'

***

Landa set her trowel and brush down, dabbing her forehead with a handkerchief. The blinding Cyprus sun made her blink several times as she smiled at her aunt, several metres away in an upright position in a three-foot hole.

'You better head back to the lodgings, Landa,' Aunty Jos said.

'It's too early, and I'm enjoying myself too much.'

'And don't I know it, Dr Landa Hayes.'

'I want to do as much as possible before Chris arrives and then Mum and Dad the day after tomorrow.'

'Well, I'm just saying. I wouldn't want you to look sunburnt in your wedding photos; the family will blame it all on me.'

'No one can do that, Aunty Jos, because I'll defend you until the sun sets and rises again.'

Her aunt laughed out loud. 'Hmm, that's our family strength shining through. Well, you might like to know that even I'm excited that the whole family will be together again in one place, and it's about time, too.'

'And that from you is saying a lot, Aunty Jos.' She smiled, beaming. 'Thank you—for everything. It's taken a few years, but Mum's back on her feet and reunited with Dad. I'm doing what I love best and marrying the love of my life. You're the best aunty in the world.'

'Well, actually, I'm your only aunt.'

''Yes,' Landa said, smiling, 'but you're still the best.'

The End.
  Tomorrow's Beginnings © Kemi Kotun.

10. THE DRIGLAIR LEGACY

The journalist wrote in the London Reporter in February 1840.

The people of Driglair live like a clan, a remnant of a settlement centuries ago; they are from the farthest north of England before you step across the border to Scotland. A genteel lot: kind and humorous – bygone characteristics that would seem out of place in a cold and soulless place like London. The few days I spent there made me a changed man – less aggressive and self-centred. The only exception was the Mayor, Ethan Leathcliffe – a greedy, self-preserving, pretentious man. If you ever visit Driglair – avoid him.

'Huh,' the mayor, Aidan Leathcliffe, said as he threw his newspaper down, 'that was fifty years ago. Papa was not amused. I will only allow journalists I know will be favourable towards us because they taste our hospitality, smile, and then proceed to pen inflammatory articles, spoiling our reputation. That's why I don't give interviews, and the penalty will be severe if anyone in this town gives one, too.'

'Yes, darling, but why are you reading that old article?' Adrinna, his wife, popped succulent dates into her tiny mouth, pursing red lips as she made a sucking sound each time.

He sipped his brandy. 'There's been an ... undercurrent...something ominous for months now, but I can't put my finger on it— it's like something bubbling under the surface. I must be watchful and tough like Papa was after the article was published years ago.'

'There has never been an unrest, but I think the Drigliarians of today aren't as temperate as their fathers.' She pushed back her dark curls, her plump cheeks glistening under the lights of the opulent chandelier.

'Something's wrong,' he persisted, 'they are quiet but cunning people.'

'Don't scare me, darling—'

'Oh no, my dear,' he looked at her pale face, 'never.'

She sighed in relief.

He continued, 'Nothing *can* happen to us; our family has held the mayoral seat here for centuries; it's an all-powerful, ruling role that my illustrious grandfather left me and my father as a legacy. We are the rulers of Driglair, and our son, Warren, will take over from me when the time comes.'

She nodded. 'Yes, my baby is coming of age; I'm so proud of him.'

He nodded, his thin, oiled moustache curled as if it had a life of its own, appearing dark against his smooth, tanned skin.

'They can't touch us; we are an institution. We *are* Driglair.'

***

'What do you mean, it's gone?' Aidan Leathcliffe half rose from his chair at the dining table, his food forgotten.

His wife placed her fingers on his arm; her single pearl ring, surrounded by encrusted diamonds, caught the light and exploded into minuscule floating fireflies.

'Sit down, darling; maybe once you've heard the whole story, it won't seem so impossible.'

She spoke with a cultured London accent, never ceasing to tell anyone who would listen about her sacrifice in moving from the fashionable and vibrant city to this out-of-the-way minuscule village the locals called a town. All for love, she reminded the mayor when she wanted yet another diamond, fur stole, or a new outfit.

"It has its advantages being the mayor's wife," she had written her sister, who was ensconced in London's fashionable Mayfair, "but the acting...the pretending to like the people of Driglair is wearing me down, and I'm so bored."

The mayor looked down at his wife as if she were a stranger, his eyes staring.

'I'm in no mood to be placated, Adrinna. Do you know what this means?' He stepped away, and she dropped her hand hastily.

Moving towards the door, he gestured to the bearer of the news to follow him. They walked through a corridor with soft, thick pile carpeting and luxurious green brocaded walls covered with paintings of the previous mayors alongside Renaissance paintings by the Masters.

'Come, Mr Kosslin, come,' the mayor turned to the man following him who had stopped to look at one of the paintings, 'surely this is not the time to muse; Driglair is under attack.'

'Surely, that is overstating it, Mr Mayor.' Kosslin said. He was a tall, broad-shouldered man with thick, light brown hair flecked with greys, which he ran his fingers through as he spoke. 'I'm born and bred in Driglair, as you know, and we have been through some rough times in the sixty years I've lived here...this doesn't compare to other trials we've come through.'

Kosslin thought he saw him raise his eyebrows in exaggeration.

'Yes, yes—' the mayor sounded bored as he turned and continued forward, '—so you keep saying, Kosslin, that everyone except I was born and bred here. I know your history as spokesman for the Driglairians and your father and his father, but I wish...' He was out of breath as he stopped and held his rotund stomach with plump fingers.

''Are you okay, Mr Mayor?' Kosslin asked in his slow drawl as he came to a standstill behind him.

The mayor waved his hand. 'Yes—yes.'

He started moving again, slower this time, as his breathing normalised.

At the end of the passage, the mayor turned left and entered a room lavishly furnished in various shades of blue: royal, lapis lazuli, navy, and baby blue.

The mayor sat abruptly on a dark blue leather sofa, making a whoosh sound, and spoke without a preamble.

'Now, Kosslin, I want to hear this ridiculous story from the beginning.'

Andre Kosslin looked at the mayor, masking his disdain for this 'self-proclaimed' ruler. He was like a stain on Driglair: himself, his father, and his grandfather. Kosslin rued the day the fine people of Driglair had first elected a Leathcliffe—it was a stain never to be removed.

He looked at the mayor now from under his lashes.

'Do you mind if I sit first, sir?' he asked, trying to lift his lips into a smile.

'Of course,' he gestured carelessly.

'There's not much to tell, sir,' Kosslin began as he took in his luxurious surroundings. His temperature rose, and his voice grew more profound with the effort to stay in control; he drew a strange look from the mayor. 'Although what there is is quite strange,' he continued as he tried to sit straight on the soft leather sofa. 'This morning, we all woke up to the excited shouts of young ones: something was missing from the town square. They were too shocked and couldn't explain what it was until we, the adults, went to find out.'

The mayor's eyes widened. 'Well, Kosslin,' he said impatiently, his thick, bushy brows drew upwards.

'It was the statue, sir, the one we call *Woman of Grace*; it wasn't there...gone, disappeared as if it never was.' Kosslin's voice drifted away. 'We were so shocked that we could only stare at the place where it had stood for over a hundred and fifty years.' He stopped speaking as the mayor held his chest. 'Are you all right, Mr Mayor?'

The mayor nodded, replying breathlessly. Continue, Kosslin.'

'As more people moved towards the square, a young girl called Mary-Jane stepped forward as we gathered around the vacant plinth. She said she had noticed the vacant space a day ago but had said nothing because nobody else seemed to notice. But after she spoke up, more people said the same thing...'

The mayor made a funny sound in his throat, which Kosslin thought sounded like he was struggling to swallow.

'...it seems that because it had been there for so long, its absence didn't register with them; I think that on a subliminal level, they noticed it but were in denial – so no one said anything.'

The mayor shook his head in disbelief, his face reddened.

'How can a statue of that height and weight just disappear – it was around five feet tall and a hundred to two hundred pounds – we're not talking about paperweight, Kosslin.' He took a deep, shaky breath. 'I don't need to tell you that it was an antique worth millions of pounds and priceless. And someone has waltzed into town and stolen it from under our noses.'

'I know it's an antique, sir. According to my great-grandfather, it was gifted to us by the people of Durruming after we helped the Gwerliche clan; it was a bloody battle, and this was their token of appreciation, made from the finest material.' He looked the mayor in the eye. 'My grandfather, who, as you know, was second in command to the then king, said the board voted to place it in the square for all to enjoy and not in the confines of the palace where no Drigliarian would be able to enjoy it—'

'That's why their roles were all abolished,' the mayor spoke disdainfully, his mouth twisted, 'because of their ridiculous policies and decisions which have made Driglair a poor substitute to all our neighbours today.'

Kosslin looked down and bit his tongue.

'Who could it be, Kosslin? Who would want to come to this remote little town to steal a statue that has been here for ages?'

Kosslin frowned at his emphasis on 'little'.

'Bromwell will know,' the mayor continued, hope suddenly inflected his voice. 'Bromwell knows everything – nothing escapes him.'

He moved toward the table and rang the bell, missing the disdainful look on Kosslin's face.

'Bromwell,' Kosslin said under his breath. The slime of Driglair, a loyal servant and hypocrite. His ancestors had served past kings of Driglair and sat at their tables, but their descendant Dev Bromwell had wormed his way into the mayor's household and 'faithfully' served him, ascending to be his right-hand man, fixer, servant, friend...whatever was required.

The mayor broke into Kosslin's thoughts. 'Yes, Bromwell will know what to do; no problem, Kosslin is too big or small for him.'

'And don't I know it?' Kosslin said to himself.

'You were saying, Kosslin?' The mayor asked with his head to one side, his eyes challenging.

'Nothing.'

There was a knock at the door.

'Come,' the mayor shouted.

Bromwell walked in. He was thick-set and dressed in a dark suit. His shoulders filled out his well-cut jacket, and his muscles rippled beneath the smooth material.

Before Kosslin's face flashed the memory of Jack Riller's injuries, the town money lender who was beaten to a pulp and left just outside of town two years ago – he refused to say who had inflicted the severe beating on him. Still, everyone knew who had, and the whispers were carried on the wind around town, instilling a fear-filled atmosphere. Jack Riller never spoke of it, but Kosslin knew everything that happened in Driglair, from the ant that crawled into the village to the adulterers' secret rendezvous outside the town to the money lender's clients...

'You called sir,' the slightly greying man in his fifties said in a deep timbre voice.

'Yes, Bromwell, we have a very serious problem here.' The mayor said. He explained the situation and asked Bromwell who he thought might be responsible.

As usual, Bromell had a few answers.

'A group of historians were in Driglair last week; they explored the town and left three days ago. They could have planned and stolen it knowing its value.'

He turned and looked at Kosslin for the first time since entering the room, his eyes holding his gaze.

Kosslin met cold grey eyes and felt his temperature drop despite the fire roaring in the huge fireplace. He held his breath. One day, he would show this man his appreciation – physically.

'Also, the second party,' Bromwell continued, looking back to the mayor, 'that might be suspects are the members of the International Antiques and Artifact Society, who visited last month. They took a great interest in the *Woman of Grace and the Black Lynx*, but I think their principles would be well above committing this crime.'

As he finished speaking, a youth in a black and white uniform walked in; he moved towards Bromwell and whispered in his ear. He gasped and hurried to the mayor's side, whispering.

The mayor stared at him; he had turned a putty colour. He stood and then sat back down and slumped.

The mayor turned to Kosslin.

'Kosslin, it's worse than we thought. Not only has the *Woman of Grace* been stolen, but so has the *Black Lynx*. Someone or...whoever is taking us, the people of Driglair, for fools, stealing our monuments from our midst.' His expression was thunderous. He thumped the arm of his chair several times. 'I want them found, Bromwell, and proper punishment administered.'

***

The citizens of Driglair were concerned about the thefts of their two monuments. The town was abuzz with theories; the main one was that perhaps the mayor had finally run so low on funds because of his lavish lifestyle with his fancy wife and spoiled brat of a son that he had sold the monuments from under them.

The typical peaceful atmosphere ruptured as they gathered in groups, searching every corner of town and spilling into the neighbouring village of Raldamir. Daily routines were forgotten as they focused on finding the lost property.

Driglairians lived in small bungalows; the women did the housework and traded, while the men either farmed or carried on the traditions of their forefathers as blacksmiths, builders, bakers and potters, doctors, and shoemakers.

They earned just about enough to keep their families above water, but strangely enough, they never complained. This was despite the extravagant lifestyle of the mayor, his family, and friends, or rather those referred to as the "rich lairs"—they all lived in royal splendour.

When the Driglairians gathered in each other's houses for their fortnightly meetings, a tradition passed down through the generations to discuss their plight and find solutions to issues, they always ended with, "Our patience will be rewarded...one day."

**

Three weeks had passed without news of the monuments. The mayor had addressed the people of Driglair in the town square weeks ago, promising to find and return them to their rightful places. He was now deflated.

'The longer it takes, the certainty they will not be found,' he said forlornly to his wife. 'I look like a complete fool.'

She laid her hand on his arm. 'You are doing your best, my darling. If those stupid people don't know that, you're not responsible. I personally don't know why you care so much about what they say,'

He looked at her. 'The people are moaning...quietly as they do, about me, under their breaths. It feels like a volcano about to erupt.'

'Yes, my sweet, but it never does–'

'I've had no trouble except with the occasional agitator, but I wonder whether this might be different; it could be the catalyst for the implosion of this anger they never portray.' He sat down. 'Tomorrow is the unveiling of my statue, which I commissioned two years ago. Do you think this is untimely, my dear? It's made of expensive material and by a famous sculptor. I wanted the people of Driglair to remember me as their great leader long after I'm gone. I wonder how they will react?'

'You worry too much, my husband.' She smiled languidly, getting off the sofa slowly, 'I must go and look for what to wear – I want to look stunning as usual.' She kissed his cheek and swept out of the room with a flourish.

The mayor called Bromwell, instructing him to increase the number of men searching; he also requested help from neighbouring towns and then sat and waited because there was nothing else he could do.

***

After a fitful night's sleep, the mayor woke in a cold sweat the following day. He turned to his wife, who snored gently and decided not to wake her. He knew she was oblivious to the money issues or how he came up with the means to pay for her exorbitant lifestyle—if only she knew.

He rang the bell for his tea; he couldn't understand why he felt so unsettled; after all, the Drigliarians had never given him any trouble.

Funny, he thought, and not for the first time, how they hadn't complained when he raised taxes or went through the streets with his wife in pomp on their way to celebrate festivities with the neighbouring towns. He knew they weren't stupid and were fully aware of his significant yearly expenditure, which enabled his family to have such an opulent existence. It was possible that they even knew he was borrowing money to stay afloat. Thank goodness for Bromwell, who helped put a certain moneylender in his place; the man's shoes were too big for his feet.

Ah, but that spooky feeling persisted.

***

The mayor unveiled his shiny emerald-green statue in the town centre amidst heavy security.

Drigliarians observed it with awe and admiration.

The mayor, his wife, and his entourage moved towards the town hall, where a lavish lunch was laid out. Only the aristocrats were invited, and they trailed behind in expensive carriages.

Everyone else went back to work.

***

Later, on the following day, the mayor's statue was reported stolen.

There was no reaction from the Drigliarians this time.

The mayor, however, went into a meltdown.

***

2 am.

The day after the mayor's sculpture disappeared, all the artisans of Driglair—the blacksmith, goldsmith, potterer, and sculptor—were hard at work, cutting, moulding, and carving.

They worked silently, each putting his heart and soul into his work in an atmosphere of camaraderie and respect.

They had been working hard each night for three weeks without ceasing, and their efforts yielded beautiful results.

***

The mayor intensified his investigations; he was by now completely mystified. Even his loyal and dependable Bromwell was at his wits' end – starting and ending with nothing.

He stood at the fashionable floor-to-ceiling windows ordered from France by his late father and looked out onto the vast gardens designed by the in-demand high-society landscaper.

Once again, he knew something funny was happening; he could feel it in his marrow, but it eluded him.

'I'm miserable, Adrinna,' he'd confessed to his stunned wife earlier, 'I'm in a lot of trouble.'

He wasn't surprised when she didn't ask what trouble and always knew the true nature of the woman he'd married—he would pay for the rest of his life for the prize of marrying her.

Now, he wondered whether the people of Driglair would finally raise their voices. He almost cheered them on to do so because he believed he would get respite and release this intense tension.

He would ramp up the search even more; Bromwell had reported that all his leads had led to nothing, and considering his record, that was saying something. That made him afraid – for the first time in his life.

What would tomorrow bring, he asked himself? A life without his title? He dropped his chin on his chest and closed his eyes.

***

One by one, under cover of darkness, Driglairians made their way to the artisans' houses; they knew the correct order to arrive because they had rehearsed it for so long. They knew what to say if one of Bromwell's men stopped them and asked where they were headed at such a late hour, but they were never questioned because they knew the proper routes to use.

Beautifully carved objects decorated the rooms of the ordinary folk of Driglair. They were made of expensive marble such as Statuario, Carrara, Italian Venetino in grey and gold, and Indian Verde in emerald green and shiny jet black.

It wasn't a coincidence that the objects' colours and materials were the same as the grey and gold of the *Woman of Grace*, the shiny black of the *Black Lynx,* or the emerald green of the mayor's newly unveiled statue.

The elated Driglairians chatted quietly as they left the artisans' cottages with their beautiful objects. They were satisfied, and a sense of achievement filled their hearts.

Kosslin stood proudly watching as they left one by one – his plan to take back control of Driglair had begun. He would take his rightful place as heir to the throne, which the last king had been forced to surrender to the present mayor's grandfather. He, Kosslin, had hidden under the role of spokesman, just as his father and grandfather had. Soon, he would make his people proud and once again rule Driglair.

For now, he was satisfied; the joy of his people spoke volumes.

The Driglairians had triumphed, and justice had been done. He had returned what was once theirs, only this time—on a more personal level; the pieces were theirs to keep—the Driglair Legacy.

He and the people of Driglair believed that generations would inherit these ornaments and would never again be oppressed by the mayor or anyone in power—he would ensure that.

***

As for the mayor, he searched and searched, but he never found.

The End.

The Driglair Legacy © Kemi. Kotun

About the Author

Kemi Kotun is a versatile writer who crafts short stories in various genres, including suspense, romance, and contemporary fiction. Her narratives take readers across continents and showcase vibrant characters from diverse backgrounds. In addition to her short stories, she writes feature-length fiction and has contributed contemporary poetry to anthologies.

She lives in London, England.